THE JUSTICE PROJECT

THE JUSTICE PROJECT

MICHAEL BETCHERMAN

ORCA BOOK PUBLISHERS

Library and Archives Canada Cataloguing in Publication

Title: The justice project / Michael Betcherman.
Names: Betcherman, Michael, author.

Identifiers: Canadiana (print) 20190066555 | Canadiana (ebook) 20190066563 |
ISBN 9781459822504 (softcover) | ISBN 9781459822511 (PDF) | ISBN 9781459822528 (EPUB)

Classification: LCC PS8603.E82 J87 2019 | DDC jC813/.6—dc23

Library of Congress Control Number: 2019934054
Simultaneously published in Canada and the United States in 2019

Summary: In this novel for teens, high-school student Matt Barnes, whose life has been
upended by a serious injury, lands a summer job defending the wrongly convicted.

*Orca Book Publishers is committed to reducing the consumption of
nonrenewable resources in the making of our books. We make every
effort to use materials that support a sustainable future.*

Orca Book Publishers gratefully acknowledges the support for its publishing
programs provided by the following agencies: the Government of Canada,
the Canada Council for the Arts and the Province of British Columbia
through the BC Arts Council and the Book Publishing Tax Credit.

Edited by Sara Cassidy
Cover design by Teresa Bubela
Cover images by Shutterstock.com
Author photo by Claudette Jaiko

ORCA BOOK PUBLISHERS
orcabook.com

Printed and bound in Canada.

22 21 20 19 • 4 3 2 1

To Laura and Claudette

ONE

It's showtime.

Matt pasted a fake smile on his face, slipped his crutches under his arms and hopped from the bus toward the front door of the school. His right shin ached where the surgeon had inserted a six-inch-long titanium rod.

Students clustered outside, waiting for the bell. A few wore shorts and T-shirts, even though it felt more like March than the first week of June. Matt said hi to his friends, but nobody asked about his leg. After all, it had been four months since he injured it. Ancient history to them.

But not to Matt. The moment his life changed forever was permanently etched in his mind.

★ ★ ★

The rock was hidden under a layer of fresh snow. Matt had been accelerating off a turn when the tip of his snowboard jammed into it. It felt like his leg had been torn from his body. By the time the ski patrol strapped him onto the stretcher, he knew he wouldn't be playing football for months. It even crossed his mind that he might never play again. But nothing prepared him for the devastating news the surgeon delivered after the operation—that he would be a cripple for the rest of his life.

Cripple wasn't the word the surgeon had used. "You'll have reduced mobility" was the way he'd put it, but there was no point in sugarcoating it. Matt was a cripple. What else would you call someone who was going to limp until the day he died?

Matt knew that in the grand scheme of things, his situation wasn't a tragedy. He hadn't lost an arm or a leg. He wasn't blind. He wasn't a paraplegic in a wheelchair like Eddie Wilkins down the street, who'd been injured in the Iraq war. But knowing that others were worse off than him was no consolation.

★ ★ ★

The hallway was packed with students, but Matt's gaze was drawn to Emma. There was no mistaking the spiky red hair. She was talking to her best friend, Rona, an outgoing girl with a perpetual smile on her face. Emma turned, as if she sensed his presence. She caught his eye and gave him a smile that tore his heart in two.

He and Emma had been together since they were sophomores, but they'd broken up in January, after Matt got a football scholarship to the University of Southern California. Emma would be going to a local arts college in Snowden to study drama, and as much as they loved each other, they both knew the relationship couldn't survive with her on one side of the country and him on the other.

At first they had decided to stay together until July, when Matt would be leaving for Los Angeles to work out with the football team for the summer. But every time they saw each other, all they talked about was how much they were going to miss each other. "We can't keep doing this," Emma had said after another emotionally heart-wrenching evening as Matt dropped her off at her house. She leaned over and kissed him. "I'll always love you," she said softly, a tear trickling down her cheek. He watched her walk up the path. When she got to the front door, she turned and waved, then disappeared into the house. It was a long time before he was able to drive away.

Ten days later he lay in a hospital bed with his leg up in traction and his life up in smoke. Emma spent a couple of hours with him every day, binge-watching *Game of Thrones*. She gave him three weeks to get used to his new reality before she brought up their relationship. "Now that you're staying in Snowden," she said, "we should start seeing each other again."

He wanted that more than anything, but he couldn't believe she did too. "I don't want your pity," he said. What other reason could she have? He pictured a hideous creature lurching at Emma's side. Like the characters in *Beauty and the Beast*, only in this version the Beast would never turn back into a prince.

"It's not pity," she said, taking his hand in hers. "I love you."

Something else he wanted to hear but couldn't believe. Only in Disneyland does Beauty love the Beast.

A few weeks later Emma got late acceptance to one of the best drama programs in the country, at a small school just outside Los Angeles. You couldn't make this shit up. After everything that had happened, they were still going to be on opposite sides of the country—only she was the one who would be in California.

That's when Matt decided that as soon as school was over, he would go live with his mom in Florida. She had moved there two years earlier, after she remarried. There was nothing left for Matt in Snowden. A fresh start. That's what he needed. He knew that running away to Florida—poor choice of words— wasn't going to solve his problems. He'd still be a gimp, but at least he'd be a gimp in a town where nobody knew who he was or what had happened to him.

TWO

Matt sat in law class, oblivious to the debate about the death penalty, his eyes on the school parking lot, where his former teammates and the cheerleaders were preparing for the annual Car Wash for Cancer.

They're so damn optimistic, Matt thought. As if life was an all-you-can-eat buffet, and your only decision was what to put on your plate. And why shouldn't they feel that way? They had their whole lives in front of them, while he stared into the rearview mirror, watching *his* life recede into the distance.

If only, Matt thought for the millionth time. If only The Goon hadn't persuaded him to get in one more run before the ski lifts shut down for the day. If only the last cable car had been full. If only he had taken a different route down the mountain, even by a few inches.

If only. Then Matt would be out there with his team-mates, with the rest of his life in front of him.

If only. The two saddest words in the English language.

Mr. Darrow interrupted Matt's reverie. "What do you think, Matt?"

"Huh?"

"The death penalty," Darrow said with exaggerated patience. "Are you for or against?"

"For," Matt said. "A life for a life. Like it says in the Ten Commandments."

"That's not one of the Ten Commandments," Sonya Livingstone said dismissively from her seat across the aisle. "But *Thou shalt not kill* is. If God doesn't believe in the death penalty, we shouldn't either."

"God believes in the death penalty," Matt said.

"What are you talking about?"

"Noah and the ark. God flooded the earth because people were so wicked. Everybody was killed except Noah and his family. That's the death penalty. Big-time."

The class erupted in laughter. The sound was music to Matt's ears. It wasn't often that somebody got the better of Sonya Livingstone. She was the class valedictorian, on her way to Harvard University—and a royal pain in the ass.

The feeling was mutual.

The bad blood stemmed from a petition Sonya had organized the previous year demanding that the school spend as much money on girls' sports as it did on boys'. It would have resulted in a huge decrease in the football team's budget, which meant it was doomed for failure at a football-crazy school like Forest Hills.

Matt would have ignored the whole thing if Sonya hadn't made it personal. In an interview with the school newspaper she'd called him and his teammates *a bunch of Neanderthals who have to take their shoes and socks off in order to count past ten*. Matt had responded by getting the entire football team to come to school barefoot on the day of the vote.

Sonya had failed to see the humor, and her mood hadn't improved when her petition was signed by only a handful of supporters.

Sonya ignored Matt's Bible lesson. "If society kills in our name, then we're no better than the murderer."

"What about the Aylmer Valley Slayer?" Matt asked. The serial murderer had killed six young women in the region before he was finally caught. He had been executed the previous month. "He deserved to die."

"What he did was terrible, but that doesn't give us the right to kill him. All that does is satisfy our need for revenge."

"You wouldn't say that if a member of your family was one of the victims."

"Yes, I would. I'd want him to go to jail for the rest of his life, but I wouldn't want him to be executed."

"He didn't show mercy to those women. Why should he get any?"

"I agree with Sonya," Kerry Chang said. "The death penalty doesn't serve any purpose except revenge."

"It stopped him from killing again," Danny Sullivan argued.

"So would locking him up in prison for the rest of his life," Kerry said.

"It costs a lot of money to keep someone in prison," Danny said. "That's not how I want the government to spend my tax dollars."

"What tax dollars, dude? You don't have a job."

"That's not the point," Danny replied, but he was drowned out by the laughter.

The bell rang. "Good discussion, guys," Darrow said. "We'll pick this up next class. Remember, there are still a couple of spots available for the project in El Salvador." Darrow was taking a group of students to El Salvador after school ended to help build houses in the countryside. "It's a fantastic opportunity."

Yeah, right, Matt thought. A fantastic opportunity to spend a month working like a dog in the middle of nowhere, and pay a couple thousand dollars for the privilege.

He looked outside as he stuffed his books into his backpack. Anthony Blanchard sauntered into the parking lot wearing his University of Southern California football jacket. Matt had the same jacket. They'd gotten them at the same time, at the press conference where they both announced they had accepted scholarship offers to play football for USC.

THREE

The Car Wash for Cancer was underway by the time Matt got outside. Cheerleaders lined both sides of Grove Street, encouraging passing cars to turn into the school parking lot. Some of Matt's teammates were washing cars while others stood nearby, loudly critiquing their efforts.

Anthony Blanchard was standing with the critics. "Yo, Matt," he called.

It's showtime.

Matt hopped over on his crutches. Even though Matt was six foot two, Anthony towered over him. "Sup, AB?" Matt said, slapping palms with Anthony and the others.

"Sup, Eleven?" the other guys said. Eleven was Matt's uniform number, and it had been his nickname for years.

"Some people will do anything to avoid an honest day's work," Allan "The Goon" Baker said, looking at Matt's crutches and shaking his head in mock disgust.

Matt grinned. "Busted."

"When do you lose the crutches?"

"A couple of weeks."

It wasn't a lie, but it wasn't exactly the truth either. A week earlier the surgeon had told Matt he didn't need the crutches anymore, but Matt wasn't going to tell that to the guys or anybody else. There was method in his madness. Aside from the doctors, only his parents and Emma knew that he had a permanent limp. The pitying looks he got now, when all anyone knew was that his football career was over, were hard enough to take. They would be unbearable once everyone saw him lurching around town. Which was why he was sticking with the crutches until he was on the plane to Florida.

"You're looking bigger every time I see you," Matt said to Steve Kowalski, the team's gigantic defensive lineman.

"The man lives in the weight room," The Goon said.

"I want to be three hundred by the start of training camp," Steve said.

"Pounds or kilograms?" Matt asked. Everybody laughed.

"You don't look like you've been missing too many meals yourself," Steve countered.

Matt couldn't argue with that. He'd put on close to twenty pounds since the accident. No surprise, given that the only exercise he'd had was lifting his fork to his mouth.

"If I can't play quarterback with the extra weight, I can always be a lineman," he said. The joke got way more laughter than it deserved. So did the next one. "I've already scheduled the lobotomy."

"What's a lobotomy?" Steve said in a moronic voice. Everybody laughed.

"Let's go, guys," the team manager shouted as two more cars swung into the parking lot.

"A few of the guys are coming over Saturday to hang by the pool," Anthony told Matt before heading off to join the others. "You should come."

"For sure," Matt said, although he knew he wouldn't go. Just like he hadn't the last time one of the guys invited him to hang out. And the time before that. And the time before that.

Even though it was a cool day, Matt was sweating by the time he had hauled himself the five blocks from the bus stop to the low-rise apartment building his dad had moved into when he and Matt's mom split up six years earlier.

He put the mail—a telephone bill and a coupon offering two-for-one pizza slices—into his backpack, then headed down the empty corridor to the apartment. He gripped both crutches in his left hand and willed himself to walk normally. His leg refused to cooperate. It was as if it had a mind of its own. He watched with a combination of horror and fascination as it swung out to the side and then back in front of his body, the right side of his butt rising awkwardly with every step. His surgeon—a doofus who assured him he'd be able to live a "full and productive life"—called it a circumduction gait, but to Matt it looked like he was a drunk with a serious gas issue.

He took a shower and then forced himself to open his biology textbook. Exams were only a week away, and he had dug himself a big hole by ignoring his studies in the months following the accident. In the past couple of weeks he had managed to get his act together, but he still had a lot of ground to cover if he was going to pass.

He was struggling to understand the difference between biodiversity and genetic diversity when his mom called.

"I've got some bad news," she said. Matt's stomach tightened. "Doug's company is transferring him to Saudi Arabia to manage one of the oil fields. We leave at the end of the month."

"Why didn't you tell me about this sooner?"

"We just found out. The man who was supposed to go can't anymore because his wife has cancer. I was hoping we could stay until your graduation, but we can't wait that long." Graduation was normally at the end of June, but the school principal had pushed it back so that the seniors going to El Salvador would be able to attend. "It's only for a year," his mom added, as if that made any difference. "You can come visit us at Christmas. The company will pay for your flight."

Super. A couple of weeks in the desert. A dream come true. He stared out his bedroom window. All he could see was the brick wall of the apartment building next door. A metaphor for his future. Or was it a simile? He never could remember which was which.

"I know it doesn't feel like it now," his mom said, "but things will get better. You'll see."

"I can still lead a full and productive life, right?" Matt said bitterly.

"Oh, Matt." His mom's voice cracked with emotion. "You've been through so much. I feel like I'm abandoning you."

"Don't worry, Mom. I'll be okay."

If only he believed it.

After they said goodbye, Matt shoved his textbook aside and hobbled into the living room. He stopped in front of the cabinet that housed all the awards he had won over the years. On the top shelf sat the trophy for most valuable player in the state championship, a bronze figure of a football player on a wooden pedestal adorned with a brass plate inscribed with his name.

Anger rose as he looked at the expressionless face with its dead, uncaring eyes. He opened the cabinet, grabbed the trophy and threw it on the floor.

The football player broke from the pedestal, severed at the knees.

FOUR

Matt was leaving for school the next morning when his father came into the living room. He glanced at the trophy cabinet and then at Matt, but he didn't say anything about the missing trophy.

Matt felt a pang of guilt. In a way, the trophy was his father's as much as his. He had groomed Matt to be a quarterback since he was little. He'd coached him in minor-league football and put him through endless drills in the backyard, until throwing a football came as naturally to Matt as putting on his clothes. He would never have gotten the scholarship to USC without his dad's help.

His father had warned him not to go snowboarding. "There's a reason NFL contracts forbid it," he had said. "You worked damn hard to get that scholarship. Why take a chance you might get hurt?"

If only he'd listened.

★ ★ ★

"I know you're upset about having to stay in Snowden," his dad said.

"You think?"

"But it wouldn't have been any easier in Florida. You would have been all alone—except for your mom."

That was the point, Matt thought.

"There are a lot of people here who care about you."

"I don't want people feeling sorry for me."

"I understand. But—"

Matt cut him off. "I gotta go," he said, slipping his crutches under his arms.

"You're going to have to get rid of the crutches sooner or later," his father said gently. "I know you're worried how people are going to react, but putting it off isn't going to make it any easier."

Worried didn't come close to describing how he felt. The same scene kept running around his head on an endless loop: him staggering around town, and everybody pretending not to notice. He might as well have a sign tattooed on his forehead: *Poor Bastard.*

"Things may have changed on the outside," his dad continued, "but inside you're the same person you were before you got hurt."

Not even close, Matt thought. But as long as he was using the crutches, he could pretend he was normal. Without them he felt like a freak.

★ ★ ★

Matt walked into law class at the end of the day. He reminded himself to call Ed Armbruster as soon as he got home to see if the job at the golf club was still available.

Two months earlier Armbruster, the president of the Snowden Golf and Country Club and a huge Falcons fan, had offered Matt a summer job working in the locker room at the club. He'd turned it down at the time because of the move to Florida. The thought of talking about the championship to Armbruster and his golfing buddies all summer long was depressing, but the job paid well. With the money he'd make, he'd be able to buy a decent used car by the end of the summer.

Darrow stood by his desk, talking to a thickset man with a graying Afro and wire-rimmed glasses and wearing a blue suit. Sonya Livingstone was listening in on the conversation. Matt wondered if the man was her father, a well-known judge. Sonya was wearing her Harvard University sweatshirt— just in case people had forgotten where she was going to school next year. The bulky top couldn't hide her killer body. She was hot. There was no denying that, even if she was a pain in the ass.

The man in the blue suit caught Matt's eye. He nodded, an acknowledgment that he knew who Matt was and what had happened to him. Like everybody else in this crappy town.

"Please welcome Jesse Donovan," Darrow said after everyone was seated. "He's the founder of the Justice Project, an organization that defends people who have been wrongly convicted. Some of you may have seen him on television when the Aylmer Valley Slayer was executed."

A few heads bobbed.

Jesse surveyed the room. "You all know that in our justice system an accused person doesn't have to prove he's innocent," he said. "The prosecution has to prove he's guilty beyond a reasonable doubt. That's to make sure that innocent people don't get sent to jail. But the sad reality is that innocent people *do* get sent to jail, and it happens far more often than you might think."

Yadda yadda yadda. Matt closed his eyes. He was drifting off when Jesse's next words jolted him wide awake.

"I know, because it happened to me. I spent twenty-four years in prison for a murder I did not commit."

There was a collective gasp from the class.

"I was nineteen years old, living in Philadelphia," Jesse continued. "One night I went to a party at a friend's apartment. The next day two men were found stabbed to death in the alley behind the apartment building. Two women who had been at the party told the police they had seen me threatening the men with a knife. I was arrested and charged with murder.

"There were two pieces of evidence against me. The first was the pair of blue jeans I'd worn that night. They had dark-red stains on them. I told my lawyer they were rust stains from an old set of barbells I'd been using, but he didn't get the stains tested, so the jury believed the prosecutor when he said they were bloodstains. The second piece of evidence was a knife the police took from my apartment. The prosecutor claimed it was the murder weapon.

"It took the jury less than an hour to come back with a guilty verdict. I was sentenced to life imprisonment with no possibility of parole."

Another gasp from the class.

"Fifteen years later I got a letter from Angela Jacobson, a woman I'd gone to high school with in Philly. She'd moved to Snowden before I was arrested and had just found out what happened to me. She asked if she could come visit me. We didn't know each other that well, but it's not as if my social calendar was full." Jesse smiled wryly. "Angela looked into my case and became convinced that I was innocent. She told me she was going to get me out of prison. It meant everything to know that somebody believed in me, but I didn't hold out much hope that she'd succeed.

"Angela refused to give up. It took seven years, but she finally persuaded a lawyer to take my case. His name was Sean O'Brien. Sean did what my first lawyer should have done. He sent the blue jeans to a lab, which confirmed the stains were rust stains, just like I'd said. He also had an expert examine the knife found in my house. The expert said the blade was too short to be the murder weapon. When Sean spoke to the two women who said they'd seen me threaten the victims, they admitted they had lied, because they were afraid of the real killer. I was given a new trial. This time the jury found me not guilty."

"Why didn't your first lawyer send the jeans to the lab?" Vince Santoro asked.

"Incompetence. My parents were both dead. I was living on my own and didn't have any money to hire my own lawyer, so the state appointed one to represent me for free. Like they say," Jesse added with another wry smile, "you get what you pay for.

"When I got out of prison, I felt like I had been given a second chance, and I wanted to do something meaningful with it. I started the Justice Project, so that what happened to me wouldn't happen to others."

"You think the Aylmer Valley Slayer was innocent?" Vince asked, unable to keep the incredulity out of his voice.

"No. He killed those women. No doubt about it. But in addition to defending the wrongly convicted, we lobby against the death penalty."

"We've been debating that issue," Darrow said from the back of the room. "I'm sure the class would be interested in your perspective."

"It's simple. We don't try to answer the question of whether or not the death penalty is immoral. We're against it solely because of the possibility that an innocent person could be executed. Since 1973, 162 people have been freed from death row before their death sentences could be carried out. That's 162 people who were almost executed by mistake," he added, just in case anybody had missed the point. "And those are just the ones we're aware of. Who knows how many innocent people are still on death row?"

"Still in favor of the death penalty?" Sonya whispered to Matt from across the aisle. Matt pretended he didn't hear.

The bell rang. The class gave Jesse an enthusiastic round of applause.

"What happened to the woman who helped you?" Vince called out as everybody got to their feet.

A smile spread across Jesse's face. "Angela? I married her."

FIVE

Matt was at his locker when he spotted Emma at the end of the hallway. The memory of the first time he'd seen her flashed into his mind. She'd been in the school play— *The Crucible*—playing the role of a young girl in the eighteenth century who had been falsely accused of being a witch. He hadn't been able to take his eyes off her from the moment she walked onstage. The next day he caught up to her as they were leaving school and told her that the playwright had it all wrong, that he knew she really was a witch because she had put a spell on him. She rolled her eyes at the corny joke but said yes when he asked her if she wanted to get a coffee.

He'd had such a great time talking to her that he was late for practice for the only time in his high-school career. Coach Bennett had made him run laps in ninety-degree heat for a half hour, but all he'd been able to think about was seeing Emma again.

How would she react when she found out he wasn't moving to Florida? Was it too late for her to transfer back to the arts college in Snowden? Dream on, he said to himself as he shoved the books he needed for the night into his backpack. Dream on.

Matt closed his locker and headed for the exit. Jesse Donovan was at the front door. He spotted Matt and held the door open for him. He nodded at the crutches. "You move pretty good on those things."

"I've had lots of practice," Matt said. Across the street a bus was pulling away from the curb. "Crap. There goes my bus."

"Where are you going?"

"Home. On Bayfield."

"I'll give you a lift."

"Thanks."

"What are your plans for next year?" Jesse asked as they walked toward the school parking lot.

"I'm going to Eastern State." Matt didn't bother hiding his lack of enthusiasm. The prospect of going to his dinky hometown college after being all psyched up to go to a university that had won eleven national championships was downright depressing. Like trading in a Ferrari for a Ford Fiesta.

"Not exactly USC, is it?"

"I'll save a bundle on sunscreen."

Jesse laughed. Matt waited for him to say how sorry he was about the injury—everyone always did—but Jesse must have sensed Matt didn't want his sympathy, because he didn't say anything.

Jesse started his car and put a CD into the stereo. "Do you like country music?"

"Don't listen to it much."

"I didn't either until I went to prison. You don't hear a lot of country in North Philly. But the guy in the cell next to mine was from Oklahoma. Johnny Mickelson. He played it from morning until night. It took a while, but it grew on me. Nothing says 'I'm hurting' like country music. Johnny gave me his collection when he got out."

Jesse drove on, moving his head in rhythm with the music as the singer wailed about a wife who had left him for another man.

Matt glanced at Jesse. It was hard to believe the man had spent twenty-four years in prison for a crime he hadn't committed. Twenty-four years! Longer than Matt had been alive. All those lost years. It would be hard enough to deal with if you were guilty. But to go through that knowing you were innocent? Matt wondered how Jesse had been able to keep his sanity.

He felt a connection with the older man. In a way they'd both had their lives taken away from them, hadn't they? He had a sudden urge to tell Jesse the truth about his limp, but he pushed it back.

They turned into a strip mall and parked in front of a storefront. *The Justice Project* was printed on the door.

"I've got to pick something up," Jesse said. "Come on in. I won't be long."

Jesse held the door open for Matt, then followed him inside. He closed the front door behind him, then opened and closed it again. It was a strange thing to do. Matt pretended not to notice.

The office was small, barely large enough to accommodate three scarred desks and an ancient filing cabinet. Cardboard boxes were piled up on the worn carpet.

A middle-aged woman with short blond hair and a round face was on the phone. "Don't worry about it," she was saying. "We'll find somebody...Yeah. You too." She hung up and smiled at Jesse. "Hi, sweetie."

Jesse kissed her on the cheek. "This is Matt. Matt, this is my wife, Angela."

"We just lost one of our interns," Angela told Jesse. "Hassan Aboud got a job at the Ford plant. He was sorry about canceling at the last minute, but it pays eighteen dollars an hour and he needs the money. I could call the other people on the short list, but I'm sure they've all found something else by now."

Jesse looked at Matt. "You interested?"

The question took Matt by surprise. He hesitated for a moment, then nodded.

Jesse looked at Angela. She shrugged. "We'd need you to work Saturdays until your exams are over," she said. "Then it will be Monday to Friday, nine to five. And you'll have to supply your own computer."

"No problem."

"The job only pays minimum wage, but it's yours if you want it," Jesse said.

"I do," Matt said. The words were out of his mouth before he realized he'd just accepted a job that paid minimum wage. But it beat the hell out of talking about his glory days all summer at the golf club. Even if it meant taking the bus to school next fall.

SIX

Angela was at her desk when Matt arrived at the Justice Project office Saturday morning. She was talking to a girl with curly hair, whose back was to him. Nice butt, was his first thought. Must be the other intern, was his second. Angela waved hello to Matt. The girl turned around, following Angela's gaze.

Sonya Livingstone.

You've gotta be kidding.

The look on Sonya's face told him she felt exactly the same. "You're working here?" Sonya asked in disbelief.

"You two know each other?" Angela asked.

They both nodded. It was hard to say who was less enthusiastic about it.

"This is your desk, Matt." Angela pointed to one of two desks that faced each other. "And that's yours, Sonya."

Matt and Sonya exchanged a look. *Great.* They'd be spending the summer looking at each other.

"If you've checked out our website, you've got an idea of the kind of work we do," Angela said.

"I was blown away by the case histories," Sonya said. "The stories are heartbreaking, and there are so many of them."

Damn. It hadn't even occurred to Matt to look at the website. Meanwhile, Sonya had been all over it. *Sonya 1, Matt 0.*

"Those are just the ones we're involved with," Angela said. "More than two thousand prisoners have been exonerated across the country in the past twenty-five years. And there are probably thousands more who are still in jail."

She pointed to a pair of cardboard boxes labeled *Prisoner Applications.* "You can get started on these. We're way behind. That's one of the problems of being underfunded. We're having a major fundraiser in August. You guys will be spending most of your time working on that." Angela plunked one of the boxes on Matt's desk, and the other on Sonya's. "The first thing you have to do is determine if the prisoner qualifies for our help. It's very straightforward. He—or she, although it's usually a he—must have been convicted of a serious crime that resulted in a sentence of ten years or more, and he must have appealed his conviction and lost. You know what an appeal is, right?"

Sonya answered before Matt could. "It's a convicted person's attempt to get a higher court to overturn the verdict."

Angela nodded. "And the person must still be in prison. He can't be out on parole."

"And you only take on cases where the crime was committed in state, right?" Sonya asked.

"That's right. We don't have the resources to help people from out of state. You've done your homework."

"It was right there on the website," Sonya said with a shrug, as if only an idiot wouldn't have thought to check it out.

Sonya 2, Idiot 0.

Matt looked around the dingy office. It was depressing. So was the thought of spending the summer cooped up in this hole with Sonya Livingstone. He peered into the cardboard box on his desk. The huge pile of envelopes was daunting. Maybe he should have taken the job at the golf club after all.

"I'm going to need your computer password so our IT guy can hook you into our network," Angela said to Matt.

"Statechamps. One word. Lower case," Matt said.

"Go Falcons," Sonya said mockingly, with an exaggerated fist swirl.

Matt ignored the sarcasm and took the top envelope from the box. He was partway through the application when Jesse entered. He closed the door behind him, then opened and closed it again.

"Good morning," he said. "You guys all settled in?"

"I've started them on the prisoners' applications," Angela told him.

"Don't believe everything you read," Jesse cautioned. "All these guys will give you a song and dance explaining why they've been wrongly convicted, but the vast majority are guilty. Very few are actually innocent."

"One is too many," Sonya said fervently.

God help me, Matt thought.

"Yes, it is," Jesse said, although Matt thought he detected an amused smile on his face.

"Why does he do that thing with the door?" Sonya asked Angela after Jesse had gone into a small cubicle at the rear of the office.

"To make sure he hasn't been locked in."

"But he's been out of prison for years."

"Twelve years. But you go through what he did, you carry it for the rest of your life."

No shit, Matt thought.

"Jesse told us what you did for him," Sonya said. "That was amazing."

"That's what everybody says, but I got as much out of it as Jesse did. I was going through a rough period when we met. I'd been through an ugly divorce, and then my parents both died within a year of each other. I was really depressed. Fighting for Jesse gave me a purpose, a reason to get out of bed in the morning. It made me feel that my life had meaning. And that's what we all want, isn't it? To believe that our lives have meaning."

To believe that our lives have meaning. That was way too much to ask for, Matt thought. He'd settle for a reason to get out of bed in the morning.

He and Sonya spent the rest of the day sorting through the applications. Injustice after injustice—if the prisoners were to be believed. "I was framed by the prosecutor."

"My lawyer was a dope." "The cops lied in court." One case blurred into another, and before long Matt tuned out the details and focused solely on determining if the prisoner was eligible for help from the Justice Project.

Sentenced to ten years or more? Lost appeal? Still in prison? Move on to the next one.

Jesse emerged from his cubicle a few minutes before five o'clock and poured himself a cup of coffee.

"What do I do with this one?" Matt asked him. "This guy was convicted of murdering his parents. He says he's innocent, but there was no appeal because he pled guilty."

"If he was innocent, why did he plead guilty?" Jesse asked.

"The prosecutor said he would ask for the death penalty if he didn't. It happened right here in Snowden."

"What's the man's name?" Angela asked.

"Ray Richardson."

"I remember that case," Angela said. "It was front-page news because his father was the Chief's chauffeur."

Everybody in Snowden knew the Chief. His actual name was Edward Jenkins, and he'd been the town's mayor for as long as Matt could remember, until the last election, when he'd stepped aside so his daughter, Jamie, could run in his place. The Jenkins name had guaranteed she'd win, and she did. By a landslide.

Jesse shook his head. "Ray Richardson. Doesn't ring a bell."

"It was more than twenty years ago," Angela said. "Long before you got here." Her phone rang.

"Is there any new evidence?" Jesse asked.

Matt flipped through the application. "No."

"Then we can't take it. Without anything to go on, all we have is another guy who says he's innocent."

Matt tossed the envelope onto the "ineligible" pile and reached for the next one.

"That was the prison," Angela said to Jesse when she got off the phone. "You're all set to see Bill Matheson on Friday."

"Is anything happening with his case?" Sonya asked.

There's no point keeping score, Matt thought.

"The judge ordered a DNA test on the bandanna," Jesse said. He turned to Matt. "Bill Matheson was convicted of murdering his wife. A bloody bandanna was found near their house, but it was never tested. We think the real murderer's DNA is on it."

"We've been trying to get it tested for seven years," Angela added.

"Why has it taken so long?" Matt asked.

"Because the prosecutor's a complete asshole," Angela said vehemently. The crude language sounded out of place coming from her, but it underlined just how angry she was. "He's fought us every step of the way, trying to stop us from getting it tested."

"That's not right," Sonya said. "A prosecutor's role is to seek justice, not a conviction."

Somebody was paying attention in law class, Matt thought.

"That's the way the system is supposed to work," Angela said. "And that's how most prosecutors operate. But some will do anything rather than admit they sent the wrong man to jail."

"How long has this guy been in jail?" Matt asked.

"Thirty-seven years."

Thirty-seven years! Matt tried to wrap his mind around that.

"Bill could have been out on parole years ago," Jesse said. "But you can't get parole unless you take responsibility for your crime, and Bill refuses to lie and say he killed his wife."

"You mean all he'd have to do to get out of jail is say he did it?" Matt asked, incredulous.

Jesse nodded.

"And he won't?"

Jesse shook his head.

"Why not?"

"*They can have my body, but they can't have my soul.* That's how he explained it to me." Jesse shook his head in amazement.

"He must be incredibly tough," Sonya said.

That's one way of putting it, Matt thought. *He must be out of his freaking mind* was another.

"If you guys are free Friday, you should come to the prison and meet Bill," Jesse said.

"Works for me," Sonya said. "My last exam is Thursday."

"Me too," Matt said.

"Great," Jesse said.

He and Angela went into his cubicle.

"Cool," Matt said to Sonya. "I've never been to a prison before."

"*Cool?* We're going to see an innocent man who has been in prison for thirty-seven years, and all you can say is *cool?* Like you've been invited to a tailgate party."

"I am so happy we're going to be working together all summer."

He had just taken another envelope out of the box when Angela emerged from the cubicle. "It's past five. You guys might as well get going."

Matt tossed the envelope back into the box.

"I'm going to stay and finish up," Sonya said.

Matt retrieved the envelope. No way he was going home before Sonya. Not even if it meant staying in the office all night.

SEVEN

What is the term for a vague or indirect expression that is substituted for one that is harsh or blunt? (1 mark)

Euphemism, Matt wrote. Like when the surgeon told him he would have "reduced mobility" instead of calling him a cripple. Matt moved on to the next question. It was the last on the exam.

What is pathetic fallacy?

Matt was racking his brain for the answer when Mr. Jolly clapped his hands. "Pens down."

That's it, Matt thought. High school is officially over.

He was confident he'd done as well on this exam as he had on the others—just well enough to get by. It was the way he'd operated all through high school. His teachers had always been after him to do better, but there'd been no point. College football coaches were interested in his smarts on the field, not in the classroom. He'd put in the time to make sure his grades were high enough to get him into university, but that was it. Doing more than that was a waste of time.

Brian French was at his locker, talking to his longtime girlfriend, Jenna Wright. Matt joined them.

"I can't believe we're done," Brian said.

"People are always saying that high school is the best time of your life," Jenna said. "If I thought that was true I'd kill myself," she said.

Matt laughed, although in his case it was probably true.

He was emptying the contents of his locker into his backpack when a familiar voice interrupted him.

"Sup, Nineteen?"

A shiver went down his spine. Over the years Emma had called him by just about every number except eleven, the one that was actually his. It was her way of mocking the school's obsession with football.

"Hey," Matt said, turning around. Emma was wearing the hoop earrings he had bought her the year before for her seventeenth birthday. "Was that your last exam?"

She nodded. "You?"

"All done. When do you go to the lake?" Emma's family had a vacation home two hours north of Snowden.

"Tomorrow."

"You working at the marina again?"

"Just for July. I got a summer job with a theater company in California. I leave the day after graduation."

Don't go, Matt silently begged. "Look out, Hollywood."

"Yeah, right. When are you going to Florida?"

"I'm not. Doug got transferred to Saudi Arabia. He and my mom are moving there in a couple of weeks."

"You mean you're staying in Snowden?" Emma was clearly taken aback.

"Ironic, isn't it?" He put what he hoped would pass for a bemused smile on his face.

It didn't fool her for a minute. Emma had always been able to read him like a book. "It'll be okay here," she said, placing her hand on his arm. "You'll see."

"For sure," he said with a shrug that was doubtless as unconvincing as the smile.

"When do you get off the crutches?"

He hesitated for a moment, but he couldn't lie to her. "I haven't needed them for a while."

"Oh, Matt," she said softly. "It can't be that bad."

He pointed to the classroom across the hall. When they got inside, he closed the door and handed her the crutches. He lurched toward the window.

When he turned back, her eyes were wet.

"Yeah," he said.

"I don't know what to say."

He prayed she wouldn't start crying, knowing it would set him off.

"Do you want to talk about it?" she asked.

Part of him wanted to let go, to vent his rage, to express his grief. But what was the point? There was nothing Emma could do.

It wasn't that he hadn't shed any tears. He'd shed plenty of them, cried himself to sleep every night for the first month after the accident. But all those tears hadn't changed a thing then. And they wouldn't change a thing now.

He looked at her sadly and shook his head.

Emma gave him an understanding nod. "I'll call you in a few days." She touched his cheek softly. Then she walked out of the room and closed the door behind her.

He took a couple of minutes to pull himself together, then slipped his crutches under his arms and headed for the door.

A large mural depicting the team's victory parade down Park Street after the state championship was painted on the wall opposite the school office. Matt was standing on a flatbed truck, surrounded by his teammates, holding the championship trophy over his head. The sadness that always swept over him when he looked at the mural was more intense than ever. At least this was the last time he'd ever have to look at it, he thought.

Pathetic fallacy. The definition popped into his head as soon as he stepped outside. *When the weather reflects the mood of the story.* If this were a story, the sky would have been full of heavy dark clouds.

In reality, it was a perfect summer day. The sun shone so brightly that Matt almost lost his balance going down the stairs.

EIGHT

Jesse was standing beside his car, smoking a cigarette, when Matt came out of his apartment building the next day. Sonya was in the back seat.

Jesse looked guiltily at his cigarette. "Don't tell Angela. Going to prison always gives me the creeps. But it'll be good to see Bill. I haven't seen him in a long time."

"I guess he'll be excited when you tell him the news."

"Not really. When you've been inside as long as he has, hope is a luxury you can't afford." Jesse took a final drag and stamped out his cigarette. "How much longer do you need the crutches?"

"Not long," Matt answered.

He could hang on to them for a week, maybe two, but that was it. And then his nightmare would begin.

★ ★ ★

Pembroke Valley State Prison was straight out of the movies. A chain-link fence topped with barbed wire surrounded a collection of squat, ugly buildings. A tower rose up at each corner, manned by an armed guard with a rifle.

Jesse, Matt and Sonya entered the visitors' center, a one-story, red-brick building separated from the rest of the prison. Matt's leg ached after the three-hour drive. They were greeted by a monotone voice on the PA system. "Visiting hours are now over. All visitors must leave the building immediately. Visiting hours are now over. All visitors must leave the building immediately."

Matt gave Jesse a quizzical look. "Bill is our client, so the regular visiting hours don't apply to us," Jesse explained.

The visitors, mostly women, slowly filed past them, chatting to each other in subdued voices. An elderly woman with short gray hair approached Jesse. "Excuse me," she said. "You're Jesse Donovan, aren't you?"

"I am."

"I'm Jolene Richardson. Ray Richardson's my grandson."

The name Ray Richardson was familiar, but Matt couldn't place it.

"You sent us a letter saying you couldn't take his case." The old woman dug into her purse and handed a piece of paper to Jesse. He read it quickly and gave her a sympathetic look.

"I wish I could help you," Jesse said. "But your grandson pled guilty, and without new evidence there's nothing we can do."

The guilty plea jogged Matt's memory. Ray Richardson had pled guilty to killing his parents. His father had been the Chief's chauffeur.

"You've got to help us," Jolene pleaded. "Ray's innocent. He loved his parents. He would never have harmed them. You're our only hope. If you don't help Ray, he's going to die in jail."

"I'm sorry, Mrs. Richardson. I truly am."

Jolene's shoulders sagged. Then she straightened, summoning her dignity. "I understand. Thank you for taking the time to talk to me."

"The poor woman," Sonya said as Jolene trudged away. "She reminds me of my grandmother. Isn't there anything we can do?"

"I don't mean to sound cold," Jesse said, "but we can't take on the case just because she says her grandson is innocent."

The guard at reception examined their identification and then handed them their visitor passes. "Pin these to your clothes," she said. "I'll call the cellblock and tell them to bring Bill down."

They walked to an airport-style metal detector at the far end of the room, emptied their pockets and put the contents on a tray. The metal detector beeped when Matt passed through.

The guard ran a wand up and down his body. It sounded when he got to his leg.

"I have a metal rod there," Matt explained.

"Roll up your pant leg," the guard ordered.

Matt did as he was told. Even after all this time, the sight of his leg—pale, scarred and withered from inactivity—came as a shock. Jesse and Sonya gawked, unable to avert their gazes, as if they were watching a horror movie on TV.

Once they had cleared security another guard led them to the interview room. "Bill will be here in a minute. Make yourselves at home."

Matt wondered if the guard was joking. The interview room couldn't have been less homey. Four black metal chairs and a black metal table sat on a gray concrete floor, surrounded by bare cinder-block walls painted a color best described as puke.

A couple of minutes later a different guard escorted Bill Matheson into the room. Bill had to stoop to get through the doorway. Matt guessed he was about six foot eight. A smile broke out on the old man's lined face when he saw Jesse. The two men hugged. Jesse's head barely came up to Bill's chin.

Jesse introduced Matt and Sonya, then told Bill the judge had ordered a DNA test of the blood on the bandanna. As Jesse had predicted, Bill didn't have much of a reaction —even though it meant he might finally get out of jail.

"It's about time," was all he said.

"Do you want me to get in touch with Heather?" Jesse asked.

"Not yet," Bill said with a sad shake of his head. "Not until this is all over."

Matt and Sonya looked at each other. *Who's Heather?*

Jesse and Bill chatted for another twenty minutes. Then Bill said he was tired and wanted to go back to his cell. He slowly got to his feet, lumbered to the door and knocked.

Matt felt an indescribable sadness as he thought of all the years the old man had spent behind bars, mixed with profound respect for the strength of character that had compelled him to turn down the opportunity to go free. *They can have my body, but they can't have my soul.* Bill might look frail, Matt thought, but inside he must be tough as nails.

"Excuse me, Mr. Matheson," Sonya called out as the guard opened the door. "Do you know Ray Richardson?"

"Known him ever since he got here."

"Do you think he's innocent?"

"I'd stake my life on it," Bill said in a firm voice.

Sonya turned to Jesse after the guard had led Bill away, but he cut her off at the pass. "We still can't take the case," he said.

"Why not?"

"Even if Bill's right, and I wouldn't bet against it, we don't have any evidence. We would have to hire an investigator to start from scratch, with no guarantee he'd be able to find anything that could help Ray."

"So it all comes down to money? If Ray was rich, he could hire an investigator to start from scratch."

"Unfortunately, that's the way the world works."

"We'll have money after the fundraiser."

"You're a real bulldog, aren't you?" Jesse said, not unkindly.

More like a pit bull, Matt thought.

"We're going to have to use the money we raise to investigate cases where we already have some evidence and where there's a good chance we'll find more," Jesse said. "And believe me, we've got more of those than we know what to do with."

"And meanwhile Ray rots away in prison," Sonya said.

Jesse shrugged helplessly. He stuffed his papers into his briefcase. A guard escorted them back to the waiting area.

"Who's Heather?" Matt asked Jesse as they walked to the car.

"Bill's daughter. She was fifteen when he went to prison. All her life she's believed that her father killed her mother. She told her children he was dead. When she finds out he's innocent, it's going to be a real shock. She and her kids are victims of this whole thing too."

Jesse tuned the radio to a country station. The hurting music suited the somber mood. Matt thought about Bill Matheson, cooped up in his cell where he'd spent the past thirty-seven years. Life isn't fair, he thought. A stab of pain sliced through his leg as if to underline the point.

"Let *us* investigate," Sonya blurted out from the back seat.

"Say what?" Jesse said.

"Let Matt and me investigate Ray's case." She looked at Matt, raising her eyebrows. *Are you in?* It felt more like a challenge than a question. He nodded. "Maybe we can come up with some new evidence," Sonya told Jesse. "And then you'll be able to hire an investigator."

She really is a pit bull, Matt thought, but this time with more than a little admiration.

Jesse broke out in laughter. "Sorry," he said. "It's just that—"

"We're kids," Sonya said.

"Yeah. You're kids."

Matt agreed. How were a couple of kids going to get somebody out of prison?

"The worst that can happen is that we don't come up with anything," Sonya argued. "We'll do it on our own time." She looked at Matt again. Another challenge he felt compelled to accept.

"That's not the issue," Jesse said. He drummed his fingers on the steering wheel. "Ok. But you don't make a move without clearing it with me or Angela first."

There goes my summer, Matt thought. But it wasn't like he had anything better to do.

NINE

Sonya was alone in the office when Matt arrived on Monday morning.

"I've been thinking about Mrs. Richardson all weekend," she said after Matt had helped himself to a cup of coffee. "Look at what she's been through. First her son and daughter-in-law are murdered, and then her grandson is convicted of killing them. She's lost everything."

Matt nodded. Sonya may be righteous, he thought, but she cares. She really cares.

"I can't wait to tell her we're going to help," she added, as if Jesse's giving them the green light guaranteed Ray's freedom.

"I wouldn't tell Ray to start packing just yet."

The night before, determined not to let Sonya get the jump on him again, Matt had combed the Internet looking for articles about Ray's case. The story of a boy who was accused of murdering his parents had made the front pages of just about every newspaper in the East. Matt had read every article, but nothing he read had convinced him Ray was innocent. He wondered why Bill Matheson was so sure about it.

Just then Jesse and Angela arrived. "You guys still want to look into Ray's case?" Jesse asked after he had gone through his routine with the door.

"Absolutely," Sonya said.

"Okay. What do we know?"

Matt jumped in before Sonya could beat him to it. "Ray's parents were murdered in their house," he began. "They were knifed to death. The back door had been kicked in, and the house had been ransacked, so at first the police thought a burglar killed them when they came home after work and found him in the house. But the next day they found a knife in the alley behind the house, and Ray's fingerprints were on it. And there were bloody shoeprints that matched his shoes, leading from the bodies to the back door."

"How does Ray explain that?" Jesse asked.

"He said his parents were dead when he came home that afternoon. He said he'd been drinking and doing drugs, and that when he saw their bodies he freaked out and ran. He claimed he didn't remember anything after that until he woke up the next morning down by the river. He went to the police station and told them what happened, but by then they'd found the knife with his fingerprints. They charged him with murder. When the prosecutor said he would ask for the death penalty unless Ray pled guilty, he took the deal."

"How did they know the fingerprints on the knife were his?" Angela asked.

"He was busted for possession the year before," Sonya said. She'd done her homework too.

"Pot?" Angela asked.

"Meth. He was only seventeen, so he got off with six months' probation."

"Did he have a motive?" Jesse asked. "Why would he want to kill his parents?"

"Ray's dad was angry at him because he was doing drugs," Matt answered. "The police said that when he came home and his dad saw he was high, they got into a fight. Ray grabbed a knife and stabbed his father. His mom got involved, and he stabbed her too. Then he tried to make it look like a burglar killed them."

"What was stolen?" Jesse asked.

"His mother's jewelry, a camera and a cassette player."

"Things that are easy to sell," Angela pointed out. "That's what a burglar would take. Who found the bodies?"

"Ray's grandmother," Sonya said.

"How horrible," Angela said.

"What do we do now?" Matt asked.

"Talk to Jolene, and then go meet Ray," Jesse said.

"What do you think of the case?" Sonya asked.

"Let's put it this way. If Bill Matheson didn't think Ray was innocent, we wouldn't be getting involved. You two have a lot of work ahead of you," Jesse warned. "The longer it's been since the crime took place, the harder it is to crack a case.

Witnesses die, or they can't be tracked down. Memories fade. Evidence disappears. Sometimes there's nothing anybody can do, not even the most experienced investigator."

There was no need to add that Matt and Sonya were a couple of rookies. The point was made. They would be wise to go into this without any expectations. Not that Matt had any.

TEN

"Did you guys read this?" Jesse asked the next day as Matt and Sonya were about to leave on their lunch hour for their interview with Jolene Richardson.

He held up the *Snowden Sentinel*'s *Sunday Magazine*. The mayor, Jamie Jenkins, was on the cover, standing on the front steps of Lawson House, the mayor's official residence. The headline was beside the picture: *An Inside Look at the Lawson House Makeover.*

"Interior decorating isn't really my thing," Matt said dryly.

"I was talking about this," Jesse said. He pointed to another headline on the magazine cover. *The Case against the Death Penalty: The Aylmer Valley Slayer's Lawyer Speaks Out. By Violet Bailey.*

"I read it," Sonya said. "It was shocking." She turned to Matt. "It listed all the countries in the world that executed people last year. The United States was the only country from

North America, South America and Western Europe that was on the list."

"Depressing, isn't it?" Jesse held the magazine out to Matt. "You want to read it?"

"Sure." Matt put the magazine in his desk drawer, and then he and Sonya headed for the door.

"Keep in mind that Mrs. Richardson is 100 percent convinced her grandson is innocent," Angela said. "It doesn't mean she's not going to tell the truth, but it's going to color everything she says." Matt and Sonya nodded. "Do you have the recorder?" Sonya patted her backpack. "I ordered your business cards," Angela continued. "They'll be ready in a couple of days."

Cool, Matt was about to say, but one glance at Sonya and he thought better of it.

"Let me guess," he said when they got outside. "That's yours." He pointed to a blue Honda Civic with a license plate that read *SONYA*.

"You're going be a great detective," Sonya said, deadpan.

A joke! There's a first time for everything, Matt thought.

"I had nothing to do with the cheesy license plate, by the way. My dad chose it."

"Sweet ride." Maybe he should have taken the job at the golf club after all, Matt thought. "Graduation present?"

"Kind of. My dad gave it to me when I got into Harvard. He went there, and he always wanted me to go there too."

"What if you didn't want to go to Harvard?"

"That was never an option."

"Do I sense a note of bitterness?"

"You really are going to be a great detective."

Matt put his crutches in the car and awkwardly lowered himself into the passenger seat.

"I never said this before, but I'm really sorry about what happened to you," Sonya said.

"Thanks."

"You know, I saw you play once. A friend took me to a game."

"Kicking and screaming?"

"Pretty much."

"Who did we play?"

"I don't remember, but you were really good. You scored three goals," Sonya joked, proving it hadn't been a fluke the first time.

A smile lit up her face. Matt wondered if she had a boyfriend.

Ten minutes later they were driving through Snowden's East End, a working-class area that had seen better times, judging by the number of For Sale and For Rent signs in the shop windows.

"Take the next left," Matt said, after checking the map on his smartphone. "There." He pointed to a four-story apartment building in the middle of the block.

They had just gotten out of the car when Sonya's phone rang. She checked the display. A radiant smile appeared on her face. "Hey, Morgan. What's up?...I bought the Ranger. I know it's expensive, but a good compass is worth every penny.

Can I call you later? We're meeting Mrs. Richardson…Okay, sweetie. Bye."

That answers the question of whether she has a boyfriend, Matt thought. "What's the compass for?" he asked.

"Orienteering."

"What's that?"

"It's a sport. You follow a course through the forest using only a map and a compass. Whoever does it quickest wins. Morgan and I have a big race coming up in a couple of weeks."

"Cool. How long have you been going out with him?"

Sonya hesitated for a moment.

"I know," Matt said. "It's none of my business."

"That's okay. We met last year at a competition in Boston."

"Is that where he lives?"

Another hesitation. "Yeah."

"Is he going to Harvard too?"

"Northeastern."

"That's convenient," Matt said. Harvard and Northeastern were both in Boston.

"Sometimes life works out."

And sometimes it doesn't, Matt thought.

Jolene answered the buzzer seconds after Sonya pushed it. "Come on in," she said. "Second door on the left."

The hallway was dark and gloomy. Jolene stood in the doorway of her apartment, waiting for them.

"Hello, Mrs. Richardson," Sonya said.

"Please, call me Jolene. Come in, come in." Jolene ushered them into the living room. It was sparsely furnished.

A wooden coffee table sat between a couch with faded upholstery and two matching armchairs. Family photographs hung on the wall above the couch. "Can I get you something to drink?" Jolene asked. "I just made some iced tea."

"That would be lovely," Sonya said.

Matt's attention was drawn to a large glass cabinet in one corner that housed dozens of model cars, exact replicas of the originals, down to the smallest detail—headlights, windshield wipers, dashboards with all the instrumentation. A number of the cars had their hoods open, revealing engines that looked just like the real thing. It was a strange collection for an old woman to have, he thought.

"This must be Ray and his dad," Sonya said. She was looking at a photo of a young boy and an older man standing beside a gleaming black luxury sedan. Ray's father was in a chauffeur's uniform. He towered over his son, who looked to be about thirteen years old. Ray was wearing a purple Los Angeles Lakers hoodie, a rare sight in Snowden, where just about everybody was a Boston Celtics fan.

"You're not the only one with a cheesy license plate," Matt said, pointing to the black sedan in the photo with THE CHIEF imprinted on the plate.

Jolene returned with a pitcher of iced tea and a plate of cookies and placed them on the coffee table.

"How old is Ray in this picture?" Sonya asked.

"Seventeen. He was always small for his age. This is what he looks like now." Jolene pointed to a photograph of her and an adult Ray standing beside a palm tree, the ocean in the background. Matt wouldn't have known it was Ray, and not just because of the passage of time. He had clearly taken advantage of the prison weight room. His T-shirt could barely contain his bulging biceps.

Wait a minute, Matt said to himself. How did Ray end up at the beach? The authorities must have given him a day pass, but Matt was surprised they'd let a convicted murderer out of jail. He was about to ask Jolene about it when Sonya pointed to a photo of a woman holding a baby. "Is that Ray and his mother?" she asked.

Jolene nodded. "Ray was Gwen's miracle baby. She had him after the doctors told her she couldn't have children." She shook her head sadly.

Jolene poured the iced tea and passed around the plate of cookies. "Thank you so much for coming. I know this doesn't mean the Justice Project is taking Ray's case," she added quickly, to show she understood that the organization hadn't made an official commitment. Jesse had insisted that Sonya make that clear when she set up the interview. "But please tell Mr. Donovan how much I appreciate this. It's the first ray of hope we've had in a long, long time." She smiled gratefully. If she was disappointed that Ray's fate was in the hands of a couple of high-school kids, she didn't let on.

"Do you mind if we record the conversation?" Sonya asked.

"Not at all."

Sonya put a digital recorder on the table and pushed the Record button. She consulted the list of questions she and

Matt had prepared with Angela and Jesse, but before she could ask the first one, Jolene started right in. The words came out in a rush.

"I was the one who found them, you know?" she said. Sonya and Matt nodded. "I remember it like it was yesterday. My son Walter dropped by around two-thirty that afternoon and told me he'd be back at seven to pick me up. I had dinner at his house every Sunday."

"I thought he was working that day," Sonya said.

"He was. But he had to take the mayor's car into the garage for repairs, and he picked up a replacement from the limo company around the corner." Jolene sighed heavily. "It was the last time I ever saw him.

"He was always on time, so at a quarter after seven, when he still hadn't come by, I called the house. There was no answer. I had a feeling something was wrong, so I got in a taxi and went over there. I knocked on the door, but nobody answered. I went inside and saw Gwen lying on the stairs in a pool of blood. Then I saw my son in the living room." She stopped talking and stared off into the distance, pain etched on her face as if it had all happened yesterday.

She's been living with this for twenty-one years, Matt thought. Since before I was even born.

Jolene collected herself. "I was afraid the killer might still be there, so I ran next door and called the police. Then I tried to find Ray. I phoned his friends, but nobody knew where he was. The next day the police called and said that Ray was at the station. They said they'd have him phone me once they finished talking to him. It never crossed my mind that they suspected him until he called me that night and told me he'd been charged with murder."

Her voice rose. "Ray and his parents were having problems, but he loved them, and they loved him. He would never have killed them, not in a million years, no matter how many drugs he was taking." She took a deep breath in an effort to calm herself. "Then there was that nonsense about him trying to make it look like a burglary to throw the police off the track. A pile of hooey."

"What do you mean?" Sonya asked.

"Gwen kept her jewelry upstairs in the bedroom. If Ray stole the jewelry after he killed her and Walter, to make it look like a burglary like the police said he did, why weren't there bloody shoeprints on the stairs as well as in the kitchen and the living room?"

"Maybe he took his shoes off before he went upstairs," Matt suggested hesitantly, reluctant to offend Jolene.

"I've thought of that," Jolene said, not offended in the least. "But if he was smart enough to do that, he wouldn't have put his shoes back on when he came downstairs and then traipsed through all that blood."

"Who do you think did it?" Sonya asked.

"It's obvious. A burglar must have been in the house when Walter and Gwen came home. That's what the police originally thought, but they never followed up on it. Once they found the knife with Ray's fingerprints, they decided he was guilty, and that was the end of the investigation." She sighed again. "They didn't even let him go to his own parents' funeral. Poor boy never got a chance to pay his respects."

★ ★ ★

"We'll pick you up tomorrow at nine thirty," Sonya said to Jolene after the interview ended. She and Matt were going to the prison with Jolene to meet Ray.

"Wonderful."

"That's an amazing collection," Matt said on the way out, gesturing to the cabinet with the model cars. "How long have you had it?"

"It belonged to Walter. He started building model cars when he was a boy. We'd go for a walk, and he could tell you the make, model and year of every car he saw." Jolene gazed into the past. "Ray helped build some of those cars when he was young, but he lost interest when he got older." It was clear from the way she said it that she didn't think much of the new activities that had captured her grandson's attention. "I'm saving the collection for him. It's the only thing he has left from his dad."

"What do you think?" Sonya asked Matt when they were outside.

"About what?"

Sonya rolled her eyes. "About the Patriots' chances of winning the Super Bowl. About what Jolene said. If Ray didn't leave bloody shoeprints when he went upstairs, he wouldn't have left them downstairs. Nobody's that stupid."

"You've never seen *America's Dumbest Criminals*, have you?" Matt asked. He wasn't surprised when she shook her head. Some of the moronic things criminals did were beyond belief. Matt's all-time favorite episode was about a guy who fell asleep in the house that he was robbing. Just lay down on a bed and took a nap.

But he agreed with Sonya. There was no way Ray would have walked through the blood in his shoes when he got downstairs, not if he'd been together enough to take them off before he went up.

ELEVEN

Sonya corralled Jesse when they got back to the office and laid out the flaw in the police theory of the crime.

"Let's not get ahead of ourselves," Jesse said. "Just because it wouldn't make sense for Ray to put his shoes back on after he came downstairs doesn't mean it didn't happen. People who are on drugs don't always act rationally. And there's another way to explain how Ray could have killed his parents without leaving bloody shoeprints on the stairs."

Matt and Sonya gave him a questioning look. "Picture it," Jesse said. "After Ray's parents go to work, he goes upstairs and steals his mom's jewelry and the other items. He wouldn't be the first drug addict to steal from his parents. Then he empties a few drawers and kicks in the back door to make it look like a burglary. His parents come home later, see there's been a break-in and suspect Ray did it. He comes home later, he and his dad fight, and his parents end up dead.

Ray flees, leaving bloody shoeprints in the living room and the kitchen, but none on the stairs. I'm not saying that's the way it happened," Jesse added, taking in Sonya's disappointed look, "but we can't exclude the possibility. The point is, you can't assume Ray is innocent. You have to go into this with an open mind."

Angela and Jesse spent the better part of an hour prepping Matt and Sonya for the interview with Ray. Then Angela got them started on the fundraiser.

"We're hoping to raise fifty thousand dollars so we can take on more cases," she said before assigning them their duties. Matt's job was to solicit donations for a silent auction from the town's merchants. Sonya was tasked with selling tickets for the fundraising dinner to Snowden's legal community.

Matt spent the rest of the day preparing a list of potential donors, but his mind was elsewhere. What if things had happened the way Jesse said? What if Ray was guilty after all? How would Jolene survive?

Matt's dad was working late and wouldn't be home for supper, so Matt decided to grab a burger at Charlie's Diner.

A framed copy of the front page of the *Snowden Sentinel* from the day after the championship game hung in the diner's front window. ***STATE CHAMPS! Barnes Leads Falcons to the Promised Land***.

Hard to believe only six months had passed since then. It seemed like six years. Matt felt like he was on a raft in the middle of the ocean, drifting aimlessly with no land in sight. He had always defined himself as a football player, and that was how others had defined him as well. It was a fundamental part of his identity. Matt Barnes. Quarterback. A package deal. The one didn't exist without the other.

But now he didn't know who he was. It was like he had been an actor all this time, without even knowing that he had been playing a role. And now the play was over, but he had no idea what part he was supposed to play next.

"Clear eyes," a familiar deep voice intoned from behind.

"Full hearts," Matt responded, turning around to face Anthony Blanchard.

"Can't lose," they both said at the same time.

Clear eyes, full hearts, can't lose. It was the Falcons' battle cry, borrowed from *Friday Night Lights,* a TV series about a high-school football team in Texas. Matt and Anthony had watched every episode together on Netflix.

"Sup, AB?" They slapped palms. "When do you head out west?" Matt asked.

"Sunday. Workouts start Monday."

"I'm happy for you, man."

"It won't be the same without you."

"You're going to do great out there."

"Tell me something I don't know," Anthony said with mock bravado. Matt laughed. "Too bad you didn't make it to my place last week," Anthony continued. "You missed a fun time."

"I was planning to come, but something came up."

"Something always does," Anthony said pointedly.

"I got a lot to deal with, okay?"

"That's no reason to freeze me out."

Matt didn't respond. There was nothing he could say in his defense.

"I thought we were friends," Anthony continued.

"We are."

"When's the last time we did anything together? When's the last time you even returned one of my phone calls?"

Matt shrugged helplessly.

"It killed me to see what happened to you. The day I came to see you in the hospital was the worst day of my life."

"Mine too."

"I don't get it, man. We used to talk about everything. Now all I get is *Sup, AB*. What's going on?"

Matt shrugged again.

"You've always been straight with me. Is it because I remind you of what you've lost? Is that it?"

Matt shook his head.

"What is it then? Talk to me."

Matt could see the hurt and frustration in his friend's eyes. He wanted to tell him the truth about his leg. He deserved to know. But the words just wouldn't come.

Anthony held up his hands in a gesture of surrender. "All right, man. If this is the way you want it. I'm not going to make it any tougher on you than it already is. You do what you got to do." He stared at Matt for a couple of beats and then walked away.

Matt watched him go. "Anthony. Wait."

Anthony turned around.

Matt put both crutches under his left arm and lurched toward him.

TWELVE

Matt was on his bed the next morning, playing on his phone as he waited for Sonya to pick him up to go to the prison, when Anthony texted him.

Be strong, brother. Love you.

Love you too.

Anthony had reacted to his limp the same way Emma had. Shock, gradually giving way to dismay, accompanied by a sad shake of the head and the words *I don't know what to say.*

What could anybody say? In a few days Anthony would be in California, chasing his dream, while Matt would be here in Snowden, dealing with his nightmare.

After Sonya texted that she was on her way, Matt got to his feet, checked to make sure he had two pieces of ID for the prison and limped out of his room. He resisted the urge to reach for his crutches. *Time to man up.*

His father was in the washroom, packing his toiletries

for the annual retreat held by the insurance company he worked for. "You off to meet Ray?" he asked. Matt nodded. "Should be interesting. You can tell me all about it when I get back on Tuesday. You won't be able to call me directly, but you can leave a message for me at the hotel if anything comes up."

"Okay. Have fun at the retreat."

"Fun is the one thing it won't be."

Matt lurched toward the door.

"No crutches," his dad said.

"No crutches," Matt echoed.

"You nervous?"

"A little," Matt said, in what had to be the understatement of all time.

"That's only natural. Just remember that your limp doesn't matter to the people who care about you."

"I'm still the same person I always was, right?"

His dad smiled sympathetically. "You are, even if it doesn't feel like it now. All I can say is I know you can deal with this, even if you don't think you can."

Matt shrugged. He wished he shared his father's confidence. He opened the door and walked into the corridor.

It was the first day of the rest of his life.

He was waiting on the sidewalk when Sonya drove up in the Civic. She lowered her window. "Hey. No crutches!"

Matt nodded, then hobbled around the front of the car and installed himself in the passenger seat, as self-conscious as if he were naked.

Sonya stared at him, unable to conceal her shock. "Is that..."

"It's as good as it's going to get."

"Oh my god. I'm so sorry. I don't know what to say."

You and everybody else, Matt thought. "How about 'you're still incredibly sexy,'" he suggested.

Sonya laughed weakly.

"'And if I didn't have a boyfriend...'"

"Don't push it," Sonya said with a smile that evaporated the moment it appeared on her face.

"We should get going," Matt said. "Jolene's waiting."

★ ★ ★

"Ray's going to be surprised to see us," Jolene said when she got into the car.

"Doesn't he know we're coming?" Matt asked.

"No. Prisoners can call out from prison, but they aren't allowed to receive calls."

"Do you talk to him often?" Sonya asked.

"Hardly ever. He has to call collect, and it costs ten dollars for a fifteen-minute call."

"That's outrageous."

"Don't get me started."

"How often do you see him?" Matt asked.

"Every two weeks. I'd go more often if it wasn't so hard to get there. I have to take the 8 AM bus from Snowden to get to Stittsville in time to catch another bus to the prison."

"How long does the trip take?" Sonya asked.

"Six hours each way. Like I said, don't get me started."

"Does anybody else visit Ray?" Matt asked.

"Not anymore. Some of his friends used to, back when he first went away, but after a few years they stopped going. I don't blame them. They have their lives to live." Jolene stared out the window at the fields of corn. "I'm all he has."

Jolene didn't say anything about Matt's limp as they walked from the parking lot to the visitors' center. Neither did the people who were lined up inside. But that didn't make Matt feel any less like a freak.

Sonya surreptitiously squeezed his hand. He smiled at her gratefully, touched by the gesture of support.

"ID," barked the guard manning the desk. He scrutinized their documents carefully and then handed them back, along with visitor passes and a key. "Pin the pass to your clothes, and put all your belongings in the locker."

They followed his instructions, then sat down on a wooden bench and waited for visiting hours to begin. A young woman with a tight Afro waved at Jolene before heading their way. She had a boy with her who looked to be about five.

"Hi, Corinne," Jolene said.

"Hey, Jolene."

"I see you brought the little guy with you."

"This is Antwan. Say hello to everybody, Antwan."

"I'm not little," Antwan said. Everybody laughed.

"You're right," Jolene said. "You're getting to be a big fellow. This is Sonya and Matt. They're law students working on Ray's case for the Justice Project." The first part of the sentence was an exaggeration, and the last part wasn't strictly true, but neither Matt nor Sonya felt the need to set the record straight.

"I hope you're going to get that boy out," Corinne said.

"We'll do our best," Sonya said confidently, as if Ray's release was just a matter of time.

Corinne took an action figure out of her purse and gave it to her son. "I don't like bringing him here," she whispered, "but my babysitter bailed at the last minute. He hasn't seen his father in two years. I didn't know what to tell him, so I told him his dad had been bad and was having a time-out."

Matt was wondering what the time-out was for when a voice droned over the PA.

"Visiting hours begin in five minutes. Form a line at the security checkpoint. Visiting hours begin in five minutes. Form a line at the security checkpoint."

Everybody stood and headed for the metal detector.

"He walks funny," Antwan said in a loud voice, pointing at Matt.

"Shush," his mother said.

"That's okay," Matt said. The kid was only saying what everybody else was thinking. "You're right," he said to Antwan. "I do walk funny."

THIRTEEN

The visitors' room contained about twenty square metal tables, each with four metal seats. Everything was bolted to the floor. A floor-to-ceiling blowup of a beach dominated the opposite wall. It was the same photo Matt had seen in Jolene's apartment. Ray hadn't been given a day pass after all. And barring a miracle—and Matt hadn't believed in miracles since he found out there was no Santa Claus—the photo was as close to a beach as Ray would ever get.

Jolene bought a can of Coke at the vending machine and pointed to a table. "Let's sit here," she said. The prisoners, all wearing blue jeans and white T-shirts, trickled into the cafeteria, greeted by hugs and smiles from their visitors. Ray headed straight to Jolene. He gave Matt and Sonya a puzzled look.

"Matt and Sonya are with the Justice Project," Jolene explained, handing him the Coke. "They're investigating your case."

"I don't understand. You said they turned us down."

Sonya explained how Bill Matheson had vouched for Ray, and that she and Matt were looking for evidence that would allow the Justice Project to take his case.

Ray didn't say anything. The look of dismay on his face said it all: How could these young kids possibly help him?

My feelings exactly, Matt thought.

"Tell us what happened that day," Sonya said.

They only had two hours. There was no time to waste with small talk. Matt sat up straight and focused on the conversation. Visitors weren't allowed to bring anything except eight dollars in change into the room. Without a recorder, he and Sonya would have to rely on their memories until they got back to the car and had a chance to write everything down.

Ray snapped the tab on the can of Coke and took a sip. "I got up about noon and had a bowl of cereal. Mom and Dad came into the kitchen. They had to go to work."

"What did your mother do?" Sonya asked.

"She was a legal secretary. She worked for Violet Bailey."

"The lawyer who defended the Aylmer Valley Slayer?"

Ray nodded. "Violet had a trial coming up, and Mom had to go in for a few hours, even though it was a Sunday. She reminded me that Grandma was coming over for dinner and told me to make sure to tidy up the kitchen before I left. We always had Sunday dinner together." He smiled wistfully at Jolene. "Dad didn't say a word to me. The day before, we had a big argument about my"—Ray hesitated until he found the right word—"lifestyle, and he was still pissed at me. After they left I finished my breakfast, cleaned up the kitchen and then went to my friend's apartment on Dalton Street."

"What's the name of your friend?" Sonya asked. Jesse had told them to get the names of everybody Ray saw that day.

"Mike Miller."

"Is he still around?"

"No idea. We hung out for a couple of hours, then Mike went to work and I went to a bar, the Linsmore, to watch the Lakers–Celtics basketball game."

"How could you get into a bar?" Matt asked. "You were only eighteen."

"The Linsmore wasn't real strict about stuff like that," Ray said with a smile. "The bartender, Skinny, was a Celtics fan, and I'm a Lakers fan, so we bet twenty bucks on the game. The Lakers won in overtime."

Matt remembered that Ray wore a Los Angeles Lakers hoodie in the photo of him and his dad beside the Chief's sedan.

"What's Skinny's real name?" Sonya asked.

Ray shrugged. "Everybody just called him Skinny. After I left, I ran into a guy I knew. Worm. I don't know his real name either," he said, anticipating the question, "but it wouldn't help you if I did. He got shot a few years after I came here. I bought some coke from him with the money I won from Skinny, but it must have been cut with something nasty, because by the time I got home I was jumping out of my skin.

"I saw the limo in the garage, so I knew Dad was home. I didn't know if I should go in the house or not. I knew Dad would go crazy if he saw I was high. Then I saw that the back door had been kicked in. I looked inside and saw him lying on the floor in the living room. I ran inside. Mom was on the stairs. There was blood everywhere." Ray went silent for a few moments. "I must have totally freaked out, because the next thing I remember is running down the alley. I don't remember anything after that until I woke up the next day under the bridge by the river at the foot of Delaney. I went straight to the police station."

A grim look appeared on Ray's face. "Two detectives interviewed me. Chartwell and Summers. They told me that it looked like my parents had been killed by a burglar. It never crossed my mind that they thought I did it. But by then they'd found the knife with my prints on it. I don't remember picking it up, but I guess I must have.

"They asked me what happened. I told them what I just told you. Summers asked me if I was sure I had cleaned up the kitchen. I said I was positive. I hadn't wanted to give Dad a reason to get angry with me. Summers said he was asking because the police found an empty bottle of beer on the kitchen table. I told him it wasn't there when I left the house. I said Dad must have drunk it when he got home from work.

"That's when it got ugly. Chartwell said I was lying. He said if Dad had come into the kitchen after the break-in, he would have seen that the back door was kicked in.

He wouldn't have sat down and drunk a beer. I said the burglar must have broken in after Dad drank the beer. Chartwell said a burglar will rarely break into a house if he knows someone's home, especially if it's a man, and he would have known my dad was home because his chauffer's hat was on the kitchen table and his coat was draped over the chair.

"He said there was a better explanation. He said Dad drank the beer before I got home. When he saw I was wasted, we got into a fight, and I grabbed a knife and stabbed him. When my mother came home I killed her too, and then tried to make it look like a burglar did it.

"That's when he told me that they'd found the knife with my fingerprints on it. I was in shock. I couldn't believe they thought I killed my parents. It wasn't until later, after I pleaded guilty, that I realized there were no bloody shoeprints on the stairs, so it couldn't have happened the way Chartwell said it did."

Maybe not, Matt thought, but that didn't rule out Jesse's scenario—that Ray had staged the fake burglary before he left the house.

Corinne was taking a picture of Antwan and his father in front of the beach backdrop. Matt wondered if one day Antwan would believe he and his dad had actually been to the beach.

Ray continued with his story. "Summers said he would do whatever he could do to get me as short a sentence as possible, but that if I didn't confess, it was out of his hands. When I refused, he got really frustrated and walked out of the room. Then Chartwell took over. He said this was my last chance to help myself. He said if I didn't confess, I'd get the death penalty. I told him I wasn't going to confess because I didn't kill my parents. Then he jabbed me in the shoulder with his finger"—Ray touched his left shoulder—"and said, *The needle's going right there, asshole.*"

"Imagine someone saying that to an eighteen-year-old boy," Jolene said angrily.

"The next morning my lawyer told me the district attorney was offering a deal. If I pleaded guilty, the DA would recommend I be eligible for parole in fifteen years. If I didn't, he'd ask for the death penalty. I asked my lawyer what I should do. He said it was my decision but that there was lots of evidence against me, and it would be very difficult to win the trial. I took the deal. It killed me to stand up in court and say that I'd murdered my parents, but it was the only way I could save my life." Ray shook his head. It was clear the decision still didn't sit right with him, even after all these years.

"I don't understand," Matt said. "You've been in prison for twenty-one years. Why aren't you out on parole?"

"Because the boy's a damn fool," Jolene said.

"Let's not go through that again," Ray said.

A voice came over the PA. "Visiting hours end in five minutes. Visiting hours end in five minutes."

Matt steeled himself for the walk of shame, but Ray's next words made him forget all about his limp.

"I can't get parole unless I admit to the parole board that I killed my parents, and I won't do that. I did it once and I'll never do it again. Never. Even if it means staying in prison for the rest of my life."

Holy shit. Bill Matheson's words popped into Matt's head: *They can have my body, but they can't have my soul.*

Ray patted his grandmother's hand. "I'm sorry, Gram. I can't. I just can't."

"I know," Jolene said, tears welling in her eyes. "I know."

Ray stood and thanked Matt and Sonya for coming, but he didn't say anything to indicate he harbored even the slightest glimmer of a hope that they could help him. He hugged his grandmother goodbye and joined the lineup of prisoners at the door leading to the cells.

Jolene watched as Ray disappeared through the door. "Stubborn as a mule," she said. "Just like his father."

Matt studied her lined face. She's been coming here twice a month for the past twenty-one years, he thought. Twelve hours on a bus for a two-hour visit. And unless he and Sonya could prove Ray was innocent—which was about as likely as Matt winning a gold medal in the hundred-meter sprint— she would be doing it for the rest of her life.

And then Ray would have nobody.

FOURTEEN

All the seats were taken when Matt got on the bus the next morning. A woman his mother's age stood and offered him her seat as he wobbled toward her. He brusquely moved past her as the other passengers watched the drama unfold. *I don't want your pity*, he silently screamed. He wished the ground would open up and swallow him whole.

Day two of the rest of my life.

By the time Matt got off the bus, the sky was heavy with black storm clouds. His mood matched the weather, and the stares he attracted on the two-block walk to the office did nothing to improve it.

"Morning," Sonya said when he arrived.

Matt grunted.

"You okay?"

"Why wouldn't I be?"

"Want to talk about it?"

"There's nothing to say."

Sonya appeared to be considering a reply when Jesse and Angela arrived.

"How did it go with Ray?" Jesse asked.

He and Angela were as amazed as Matt and Sonya had been when they learned that Ray had chosen to stay in jail for the rest of his life rather than lie about killing his parents in order to get parole. "No wonder Bill Matheson said he was innocent," Angela said.

Innocent and out of his freaking mind, Matt said to himself. Just like Bill.

"But this still doesn't mean we can put an investigator on the case," Jesse said, beating Sonya to the punch. "You guys are going have to come up with some evidence before we can do that."

"I know," Sonya said. "But now you believe he's innocent, don't you?"

"Let's put it this way. I've never come across a case where a guilty person has refused parole. Did you get the authorization?"

Sonya handed him the letter Ray had signed, authorizing his former lawyer to give the case file to the Justice Project.

"Who was his lawyer?" Angela asked.

"Doug Cunningham," Jesse answered, pulling out his cell phone and punching in a number.

"Doug took a table at the fundraiser, so don't forget to thank him," Angela said.

Jesse nodded. "Hey, Doug. Thanks for buying a table, man. I really appreciate it. I've got you on speakerphone.

I'm here with Angela and my two interns, Sonya Livingstone and Matt Barnes."

"*The* Matt Barnes?" Cunningham asked.

"*The* Matt Barnes," Jesse echoed.

Who no longer exists, Matt said to himself.

"Hi, Matt. I know everybody says they were at the game, but I was actually there. Great stuff."

"Thanks," Matt said. *The game.* It was all anybody ever talked about. If he never heard another word about it, it would be too soon.

"We're calling about one of your old cases," Jesse said. "Ray Richardson."

"Haven't heard that name in a long time."

"What did you make of the case?"

"I don't know. The whole thing was over in a couple of days, but Ray just didn't seem like the kind of person who could kill his own parents. Then again, if he was loaded up on drugs, who knows? I have to admit I breathed a huge sigh of relief when Lonnie put parole on the table. I was dreading the trial. I didn't think we had much chance of winning, not with all the evidence against him. Once Ray fled the scene, his goose was cooked."

"Lonnie as in Lonnie Shelton, our esteemed state attorney general?" Jesse asked, putting sarcastic emphasis on the word *esteemed*.

"He was the DA here in Snowden back then," Doug said.

"If Lonnie was going to win the case anyway, why offer Ray parole?" Jesse asked. "He's built his career on his support for the death penalty. Did you see his press conference after the Aylmer Valley Slayer was executed? If he'd had his way, it would have been done in public. Why give Ray a break?"

"Don't quote me on this, but I always thought he and the Chief made a deal. The Chief was in the middle of an election, and it was a tight race. His character had become a campaign issue. There were rumors he was playing around with other women. That kind of behavior doesn't sit well with folks in this town. Ray's case was front-page news, and every story mentioned that his father worked for the Chief. It wasn't the kind of publicity the Chief was looking for."

"What was in it for Lonnie?" Jesse asked.

"The Chief supported him the next year when he ran for state attorney general. I can't prove they made a deal, but I don't think it was a coincidence. What's Ray up to these days?"

"He's still in prison."

"The parole board turned him down?"

"He never applied."

"Why not?"

"He won't admit he's guilty."

"You got to be kidding."

It was unanimous, Matt thought. Everybody believed Ray was innocent. And it was up to him and Sonya to prove it.

FIFTEEN

Matt's dad was at the kitchen table when Matt got up on Tuesday morning.

"How was the retreat?" Matt asked.

"It was a joke. Four days of team-building exercises led by a complete moron. Last night we sat around a campfire and sang 'Kumbaya.' I kid you not. As if that's going to help anybody sell more insurance." He shook his head in disgust. "How are you doing?"

Matt shrugged. His dad nodded sympathetically. Matt was glad he didn't try to make him feel better by saying something stupid like *everything's going to be okay.*

"How did it go at the prison?" his father asked.

Matt filled him in on the case.

"If I was Ray, I'd admit to the murders on national television if it meant getting out of jail," his dad said.

"Me too."

"Those rumors about the Chief weren't just rumors," his father said when Matt told him about the suspected deal between the Chief and the DA that had spared Ray from the death penalty. "I know that for a fact, because he came on to your mother."

"What?"

"It was at the opening of the community center on Dawson, just after we were married. I wasn't there, but your mom told me about it afterward. The Chief told her she was the most beautiful woman in Snowden and invited her to the Regency Hotel to 'have lunch.'" He made air quotes with his fingers.

"What a sleazebucket!" Matt said.

"Yeah, but I can't fault him for his taste. Your mom *was* the best-looking woman in town." He got to his feet. "Time to hit the salt mines. See you at dinner."

* * *

"Doug Cunningham sent over the Richardson case file," Angela told Matt when he arrived at the office. "I put the box on your desk."

Matt grabbed a coffee and dug in. The box contained a number of file folders, each with a label: *Police Reports. Witness Statements. Forensics. Crime Scene Photos. Plea Bargain Agreement.*

Matt started with the witness statements. There were only a few, because the investigation ended when Ray pled guilty.

Only one witness had anything to report—Ella Didrickson, one of the Richardsons' neighbors. She saw Walter drive the limo into his garage at around four o'clock on the day of the murders. Fifteen minutes later she saw Gwen park the Richardsons' car in the driveway and then go into the house through the front door.

Matt moved on to the crime-scene photos. The first photo showed the black sedan in the garage. Matt noticed that it didn't have the Chief's vanity license plate. He was puzzled for a moment until he remembered that Walter had taken that car in for repairs. The car in the garage was the replacement he had picked up from the limo company near Jolene's apartment.

The next picture was an eight-by-ten-inch print of Walter lying on a blood-soaked carpet, in front of the glass cabinet showcasing the model cars that Matt had seen at Jolene's house. The next picture was also of Walter. And so was the next. And the one after that. The police photographer had taken pictures of Ray's father from every conceivable angle. He'd done the same with Gwen, who was lying facedown partway up the stairs.

There was nothing in the photos Matt hadn't seen dozens of times on TV without batting an eye, but it was different knowing that these victims were real people who had been alive a few short hours before the photos were taken. He tried to imagine how Ray must have felt, coming home and stumbling onto the gruesome scene. Anybody would be freaked out, Matt thought. And it would be even freakier if your mind was fried by drugs. No wonder he'd panicked and fled, even if that did "cook his goose," like Doug Cunningham said.

The next photo showed the back door. It was splintered where it had been kicked in. The doorframe dangled from the wall. The following picture was of the kitchen table. The empty bottle of beer that had aroused the attention of the police stood on the table beside a copy of the *Snowden Sentinel* and Walter's chauffeur's cap. Close-ups of the three items followed. The beer was a Rolling Rock, the same brand Matt's dad favored.

Walter's coat was draped over a chair that faced the back door. How could he have sat there and drunk an entire beer without noticing that the door had been kicked in? Matt asked himself. No wonder the police had been so suspicious of Ray's story.

A nagging thought intruded. Could it have happened the way Jesse suggested? Did Ray commit the burglary and fake a break-in before he went to Mike Miller's apartment? Matt imagined Walter sitting at the table, staring at the broken back door as he drank his beer, his anger building up. He would have been furious by the time Ray came home from the bar after watching the basketball game. Walter was a lot bigger than Ray, and Ray would have been paranoid because of the drugs. Matt could see how Ray might have grabbed a knife to protect himself. But if that had been the case, Ray would be out on parole, wouldn't he? A guilty person wouldn't turn down the chance to get out of jail.

Matt had finished with the photos and was starting in on the autopsy report when Sonya arrived.

"Is that the case file?" she asked Matt.

"Yeah. I'm done with the stuff in the box."

The autopsy report was full of incomprehensible medical jargon, but the pathologist's conclusions were in plain English, and they held no surprises. Walter and Gwen had both died from multiple stab wounds. There were no surprises with the forensics either. Ray's fingerprints were on the knife. His parents' blood was on the clothes he was wearing when he went to the police the day after the murder. And the bloody shoeprints in the kitchen and living room were his.

"You can take this too," Matt said after he finished reading the report. He placed it on Sonya's desk. She was staring at one of the crime-scene photos, a horrified look on her face.

"You okay?" he asked.

She looked up at him, an anguished look on her face. "Can you imagine finding your parents killed like this and then having the entire world believe you were the one who did it?" Matt shook his head. "We've got to find out who did this so we can get Ray out of jail," Sonya said.

"We will," Matt assured her. He kept his doubts to himself. As a general rule he believed honesty was the best policy. But sometimes it was just too damn cruel.

SIXTEEN

Two men were talking to Angela and Jesse when Matt came out of the washroom. He instantly recognized the older of the two, a distinguished-looking man with a craggy face and a full head of silver hair—the Chief, the sleazebucket who had made a move on his mom.

It took a moment to place the Chief's companion, a bald man with an ear stud. It was Dan Burke, husband and chief of staff to the current mayor, Jamie Jenkins. Matt had met him at a reception that Jamie had held for the team after the state championship.

Matt made his way toward the two men. They both kept their eyes squarely on his, as if they hadn't noticed his limp.

As if.

"These are our summer interns, Sonya Livingstone and Matt Barnes," Angela said.

The sleazebucket clapped a friendly hand on Matt's shoulder. Matt resisted the urge to shrug it off. "This young man needs no introduction. December 6," he said, referring to the date of the championship game. "The greatest day in the history of this town."

Matt grunted.

The Chief turned to Sonya. "Any relation to the judge?"

"He's my father."

"Please give him my regards."

"Jamie and I want to host a cocktail party after the fundraiser," Dan Burke said, "to encourage some of our more affluent supporters to pony up."

"That's very generous of you, Dan," Jesse said. "Please tell her how much we appreciate it."

"If you need any help twisting arms for donations, give me a call," the Chief chimed in, eager to let everyone know he still had clout in Snowden even though he was no longer mayor.

"Do you remember Ray Richardson?" Sonya asked suddenly.

"Ray Richardson?" the old man said uncertainly. "Why is that name familiar?"

"His father, Walter, was your driver," Burke said.

"Of course." The Chief shook his head sadly. "That was a real tragedy. Walter used to bring the boy around from time to time. He seemed like a nice kid." He shrugged. *Go figure.*

"I was probably the last person to speak to Walter that day," Burke said, "aside from—" He stopped in midsentence.

Matt finished it. *Aside from the killer.*

"Walter had to take the car to the garage for repairs. I told him the Chief had meetings all afternoon and probably wouldn't need him, but I asked him to call me after he picked up the replacement car, just to make sure. When he called, I told him he didn't have to come in." The look on Burke's face said it all. *If only the Chief had needed Walter.*

"Did you know Ray?" Sonya asked.

"No. I'd only been working for the Chief for a couple of months when it happened."

"If I'd known you were more interested in my eighteen-year-old daughter than my plans for the city, I would never have hired you," the Chief teased.

"We told you we were dating. It just took us a while to get around to it," Burke joked in return.

Matt did the math. Burke would have been around thirty when he started working for the Chief. No wonder he and Jamie had kept their relationship a secret. Sleazebucket could laugh about it now, but he wouldn't have been laughing back then. Not that he was one to talk. The age difference between him and Matt's mother was a lot greater than the age difference between Burke and Jamie.

"Why are you interested in the Richardson case?" the Chief asked. "The kid confessed."

"He did, but we think he might be innocent," Jesse said and then explained why.

"That's unbelievable," the Chief said.

"Incredible," Burke agreed. "But doesn't the Justice Project need to have actual evidence of innocence in order to take on a case?"

"Dan's right," the Chief said quickly. "We've got a fundraiser coming up. How do you think people are going to react when they find out you're using their money to follow a hunch?"

"Relax, Ed. We haven't officially taken on the case."

"It still doesn't look good. You're using Justice Project resources—phones, office space. And Matt and Sonya are out in public as representatives of the Justice Project."

"Nobody's going to care about that."

"You'd be surprised at what gets people's noses out of joint."

"The fundraiser's not for another month and a half," Jesse pointed out. "Either Matt and Sonya will have come up with something by then, and we'll be able to officially take on the case, or they'll have run out of leads. One way or another, it'll be over by then."

One way or another, Matt thought. It would take one of those miracles he'd stopped believing in for him and Sonya to come up with something.

"I have an idea for the fundraiser," Burke said. "We should auction off a state championship sweatshirt signed by Matt and the rest of the team. I bet we could get a thousand dollars for it."

"Great idea," the Chief said enthusiastically. "I would bid on that myself."

"Can you take care of getting the players to sign it?" Jesse asked Matt.

"No problem. I'll leave it at the school office and send the guys an email."

Sonya shook her head in bewilderment after the three men and Angela left for lunch. "A thousand dollars for a football jersey? There is something seriously wrong with this town."

"I agree," Matt said. "It's worth at least two thousand."

★ ★ ★

Matt had just ordered a meatball sub at the sandwich shop around the corner from the office when an attractive girl wearing a Snowden Adventure Camp Staff T-shirt joined him at the deli counter.

"What can I get you?" the server asked.

"I'm here for a pickup. Caitlyn."

The woman disappeared into the kitchen. Matt and Caitlyn smiled at each other.

"How's camp?" Matt asked.

"I haven't lost any kids yet, but it's only my second day, so I guess I shouldn't be too cocky."

Matt laughed.

"I'm Caitlyn."

"I figured. Matt."

"Do you work around here?"

"Down the street at the Justice Project. It's an organization that defends the wrongly convicted."

"I walked by it on my way here. I wondered what it was all about. That must be really interesting."

"It is," Matt said, as the server reappeared holding two brown paper bags, one small and one large. She gave the small one to Matt and the large one to Caitlyn.

Caitlyn turned, anticipating they would leave together.

She was hot, she was friendly, and she was going his way. Any normal guy would have jumped at the opportunity. *Normal* being the operative word. Matt remained rooted in place.

"See you later," Caitlyn said after a few awkward moments.

"See you," Matt said, suddenly engrossed by the contents of the deli counter. He waited until Caitlyn had left the shop before he walked to the cash register. He felt about two feet tall.

On his way back to the office he noticed a man with a baseball cap staring at him from across the street. "What the fuck are you looking at?" Matt shouted.

SEVENTEEN

"The one thing we have going for us is that there are a lot of potential witnesses the police didn't speak to," Jesse said the next day, after Matt and Sonya told him what they had learned or, more accurately, how little they'd learned from the case file.

"Where should we start?" Sonya asked.

"Start by talking to the neighbors who were living there at the time of the murder. You can get a list from the records department at city hall."

"I'll help you write up the request," Angela said.

"Tell Ralph we need the Richardsons' phone records for the day of the murder," Jesse told Angela.

"Who's Ralph?" Matt asked.

"Ralph Chadwick. One of our investigators. Get him to charge his time to one of his active cases," Jesse told Angela. "We need to keep Ray's case off the books."

"And the Chief off our backs," Angela added.

An hour later Matt and Sonya were walking up the stone stairs to city hall. Sonya pushed open the heavy wooden door. It took a moment for Matt's eyes to adjust to the darkness inside. Dark wood paneling lined the walls of the foyer. The faded wood floors were in serious need of a new coat of stain. The gloomy atmosphere underlined the daunting nature of their mission.

The records department was on the third floor. Matt was huffing and puffing by the time they arrived, and his leg was killing him. Time to hit the pool, he told himself. The surgeon had told him to start swimming—it was the only form of cardio he could do, and it would strengthen his leg— but swimming had to be the most boring exercise in the world, and Matt wasn't exactly motivated. But it was either that or turn into the Michelin Man.

A severe-looking woman sat at a desk on the other side of the service counter, tapping away at her computer. She wore a T-shirt emblazoned with the words *State Champions*. Matt reminded himself to drop off a sweatshirt at the school for the players to sign for the silent auction.

They waited for a couple of minutes before the clerk served them. "We're with the Justice Project," Sonya said, handing the woman her business card. Matt did the same. It was the first time he'd used it, and he felt like an impostor. Kids didn't have business cards. He half expected the woman to laugh.

"We need a list of residents—" Sonya began.

"All requests have to be in writing," the woman interrupted.

Sonya handed her the letter Angela had prepared. The woman clipped the business cards to the letter, returned to her desk, put the letter in a tray and started tapping away again.

"Excuse me," Sonya said. The woman looked up. "How long is this going to take?"

Longer than it would have if you hadn't asked, Matt thought. The woman shrugged and returned to her keyboard.

"Nice job," Matt said as they sat down on a bench.

"Like you could do better."

Matt stood. "Call my phone when I give you the sign."

"What are you talking about?"

"Just do it."

He went to the counter and surveyed a collection of informational pamphlets, choosing one at random. There was no reaction from the clerk. Sonya gave him a sarcastic thumbs-up. Matt held his hand to his ear, thumb and pinky extended, as if it were a phone. Sonya rolled her eyes, but she took her phone out of her bag and punched in Matt's number.

Matt's phone rang. "Hello," he said. "Coach Bennett! What's up?" The woman's head swiveled toward Matt at the mention of the Falcons' head coach. "No. I didn't get it. What email address did you send it to?...I don't use that one anymore. Send it to Matt underscore Barnes at gmail dot com...Great. See you later."

He put his phone away and started reading the pamphlet. The woman examined the request letter with Matt's business card.

"You're Matt Barnes," she said stupidly.

"Guilty."

"My son is going to be so excited when I tell him I met you. He's your biggest fan. Would it be too much to ask for your autograph?"

"Not at all." Matt gave her his most winning smile. He smirked at Sonya, who made a gagging motion as the woman rooted around in a desk drawer. She pulled out a program from one of the Falcons games and gave it to Matt.

"What's your son's name?" Matt asked.

"Jerrold. *J-e-r-r-o-l-d*." Matt signed the program and gave it back to her. "Maybe I should put this up on eBay instead of giving it to him," she joked. Matt laughed obligingly. The woman pointed at the request letter. "I'll take care of this right away."

Fifteen minutes later Matt and Sonya walked out of the records department with two printouts, one with the names and addresses of the Richardsons' neighbors at the time of the murder, and a second with the names and addresses of the people who lived there now.

"No comment?" Matt asked.

"About what?"

"About how seriously screwed up this town is."

"Go Falcons."

EIGHTEEN

Matt dragged himself out of bed on Sunday, cursing Sonya for insisting that they get to the Richardsons' neighborhood first thing in the morning.

She had shown absolutely no interest in negotiating when Matt suggested that a noon start would be ample. "Suit yourself," she said. "I'm starting at nine. You can join me. Or not," she added, a comment Matt had interpreted as a challenge, although it was equally possible she didn't care.

He put on a pair of jeans and his green-and-gold Falcons football jersey with his number on the front and his name on the back. Judging by his experience at the records department, it might help open some doors.

Sonya was standing by her Civic. It was already hot, even though it was still early. Sonya wore a sleeveless summer dress.

She looks great, Matt thought. Morgan's a lucky guy.

She glanced at his football jersey. "Man, I can't wait to get out of this town."

"How did you do in the orienteering competition yesterday?" Matt asked after they got in the car. He pushed the seat as far back as it could go, so he could stretch out his leg.

"I finished second."

"How about Morgan?"

"Fourth."

"That's embarrassing."

"How so?"

"Most guys don't like getting beat by their girlfriend, even if they wouldn't admit it. Morgan must be very understanding."

"She is."

For a moment Matt thought she was joking, but the serious look on her face convinced him otherwise. "Nobody knows, except for a few close friends," Sonya said, "so I'd appreciate your keeping this to yourself."

Matt nodded solemnly. He wasn't surprised Sonya didn't want to tell anyone she was gay. Personally, he didn't give a hoot, but Forest Hill was a conservative school in a conservative town. Sonya had taken a lot of flak for challenging football's position at the center of Snowden's solar system when she'd tried to get more money for girls' sports. She'd have taken a lot more if people knew she was gay.

"Have you told your parents?"

"I'm working up to it. My dad's old school. Having a gay daughter won't fit with his worldview."

"What about your mom?"

"She'll be okay with it. But I haven't told her, because I don't want to put her in the position of keeping a secret from my dad."

"You're going to have to tell them sooner or later."

"I know. I'm going do it after graduation. College graduation."

Matt laughed. "I guess I've lived a sheltered life. I don't know any other girls who are gay."

"Oh yes you do."

★ ★ ★

They parked across the street from the Richardsons' former home on Huntington Terrace. The house, like all the others in Cooley Park, was a modest two-story red-brick dwelling with an attached single-car garage. There wasn't a terrace in sight. Whoever named the street was trying to make the working-class neighborhood sound a lot more upscale than it actually was.

A young boy with a Mohawk haircut was riding his tricycle in the driveway while his mother watered the flowers that lined the path to the front door. Matt looked at the peaceful scene without seeing it. In his mind's eye he was inside the house, staring at the lifeless bodies of Walter and Gwen.

"I'm glad we don't have to go in there," Sonya said, as if she'd read his mind.

Matt nodded. They would learn nothing by going into the house. Everything they needed to see was in the crime-scene photos.

Jesse had suggested they retrace Ray's steps before they started knocking on doors. They headed for the alley behind the house. It was lined with weeds. Sonya stopped partway down. "This is the house," she said.

"How do you know that?"

"I counted. It's the eighth house in."

Matt smiled. He might as well get used to the fact that Sonya was always going to be one step ahead of him.

Sonya leafed through the crime-scene photos until she found one of the rear of the house. They compared it to the scene in front of them. The back door had been replaced by sliding glass doors, the garage had a fresh coat of paint, and a new swing set dominated the small backyard. Otherwise everything was the same. The same rickety wood fence separated the house from the alley, the same concrete path led from the rear gate to the back door, the same diamond-shaped window graced the back wall of the garage.

"The Linsmore is two blocks that way," Sonya said, referring to the bar where Ray had watched the Lakers–Celtics basketball game. She pointed in the direction she and Matt had come from. "Ray comes down the alley and goes through the gate. He sees the limo in the garage, so he knows his dad is home. He's wondering what to do when he sees that the back door has been kicked in. He sees his father lying on the floor in the living room. He runs inside."

Matt broke in. "I don't understand how Walter could have sat down and drunk an entire beer without noticing that the back door was kicked in?"

"Maybe he thought Ray faked the burglary, like Jesse suggested."

"If that was the case he wouldn't have cracked open a beer. He would have gone to see what Ray had stolen, and the burglar would have killed him before he had the beer."

"Maybe he was concentrating on something in the newspaper." Sonya pointed to the photo of the *Snowden Sentinel* on the kitchen table. "I'm like that. When I'm reading, I blot out everything else. It drives my sister crazy. She has to call my name ten times before it registers. Anyway, what does it matter?" she asked. She resumed her narrative. "Ray sees that his parents are dead. He panics and runs out of the house and down the alley toward Delaney."

Sonya headed off. Matt lurched after her. A step behind.

"The houses on both sides have good views of the alley," Sonya noted. "That's a plus."

"Only if somebody happened to be looking out at the exact moment the killer was in the alley. What are the chances of that?"

"Somebody must have seen something."

"The glass is always half-full, huh?"

"That's better than thinking it's always half-empty." Sonya's eyes flickered to his leg.

It's not half-empty, Matt thought. It's bone-dry.

The alley ended at Delaney Heights. The street had obviously been christened by the same person who named Huntington Terrace: it was as flat as the prairies.

Delaney was a major thoroughfare, lined with apartment buildings and small businesses. It was full of pedestrians. Once the real killer got here, he would have melted into the crowd.

Ray had turned left and gone down to the river. Matt and Sonya turned right. It was time to start knocking on doors.

NINETEEN

When they got back to Huntington Terrace, Sonya handed
Matt a spreadsheet. "This has the names and addresses of all
the people who lived in the neighborhood back in the day.
The ones in red still live here. We can google the ones who've
moved away."

Matt looked at the list. There were 163 names on it.
He gazed down the street. It was a hive of activity. People
walking on the sidewalks, tending to their gardens, washing
cars in their driveways, sitting on their porches.

It's showtime.

They knocked on four doors before somebody answered.
A lumpy woman stared out at them, a sour expression on her face.

"Mrs. Parker?" Sonya asked.

"I don't care what you're selling. I'm not interested."

"We're not selling anything," Sonya said quickly. She gave
the woman her business card. "We're with the Justice
Project. We're looking into the Ray Richardson case."

"The boy who killed his parents? What are you looking into that for?"

"We think he may be innocent," Sonya said.

"Innocent!" Mrs. Parker scoffed. "They should have strapped that monster into the electric chair."

"Do you remember where you were that day?" Sonya asked, apparently deciding to forgo the golden opportunity to debate the death penalty.

"How am I supposed to remember where I was twenty years ago?" The woman started to close the door.

"Could we speak to Mr. Parker?" Sonya asked.

"Sure, but you'll need a hell of a long-distance plan."

Sonya gave her a puzzled look.

"He died four years ago."

The door closed in their faces. "This is going to be fun," Sonya said dryly.

Donna Mills across the street looked annoyed when she answered the door, but that changed as soon as she saw Matt in his football jersey.

"You're Matt Barnes," she said, a smile spreading across her face. "But I guess you know that. My husband, Terry, and I are big fans. We never miss a game." Her face grew somber. "We were so sorry to hear about the accident."

Donna didn't have any information to contribute. She and Terry and their two kids had been at a movie. She found out about the murders when they came home and saw their neighbors congregated outside the Richardson house.

"Sorry I can't be more help." Donna turned to Sonya. "You look familiar too. You're one of the cheerleaders, aren't you?"

"Go Falcons!" Sonya said perkily.

"You were right," Matt said as they walked away. "This *is* going to be fun."

"Ha ha."

Matt and Sonya knocked on door after door. Half the people weren't home, and the other half hadn't seen a thing. Everyone was far more interested in talking about the state championship and commiserating with Matt about his injury than talking about the murders.

By eleven o'clock they had moved on to the houses on Robert Street, which overlooked the alley behind the Richardsons' house.

"Leon, Henry and Lenore Patterson," Sonya announced as they approached the third house from the corner.

An elderly woman with white hair answered the door. "Mrs. Patterson?" The woman nodded. "We're with the Justice Project and—"

"Oh yes," Mrs. Patterson interrupted. "Jolene told me about you."

"You know Jolene?" Matt asked.

"We've been friends for sixty years. I was with her when Ray called to say he'd been charged with murder." She sighed.

Mrs. Patterson hadn't seen anything noteworthy on the day of the murder, and neither had her husband, Henry, who had passed away a few years after the murders.

"Is Leon at home?" Sonya asked.

"My son lives in Rio de Janeiro. He married a Brazilian woman. I can give you his email address." She wrote it down on a piece of paper. "You bring Ray back home," she ordered. "That boy's suffered enough. And so has his grandma."

"We'll do our best," Sonya said.

For what it's worth, Matt silently added.

"This is the last house on the list," Sonya said two hours later.

Hallelujah. Matt trudged up the pathway. His shirt was soaked with sweat, and his leg was crying for mercy. Tomorrow I hit the pool, he told himself. No more excuses.

A tall man with a prominent paunch opened the door.

"Mr. Lewis?" Sonya asked.

The man's eyes widened when he saw Matt. From the look on his face, it could have been Brad Pitt standing on his doorstep.

Lewis didn't remember where he'd been on the day of the murders, but there was nothing wrong with his short-term memory, and he proved it by launching into a play-by-play analysis of the championship game. He was halfway through the first quarter before he took a breath, giving Matt an opportunity to terminate the conversation.

"Gee, just when it was getting interesting," Sonya said as they headed to the car.

"I can finish up, if you'd like."

"I'd rather you pulled out my fingernails with a pair of pliers."

Matt laughed.

"You should run for mayor," Sonya said. "You'd be a shoo-in."

"I'd get the sympathy vote, that's for sure."

Sonya gave him a sideways glance but didn't say anything.

The car was as hot as a furnace. Sonya lowered the windows and took a sandwich out of her backpack. "Didn't you bring anything to eat?"

Matt shook his head.

She reached into her bag. "I have an extra sandwich."

"That's okay. I'll grab something at home."

"We're not done. We've got to go back to the houses where nobody answered."

The prospect of a few more hours under the hot sun had about as much appeal to Matt as walking barefoot on a bed of nails, and it must have shown on his face.

"Is your leg sore?" Sonya asked. "I can take you home if you need to rest."

Matt held out his hand. Sonya passed him the sandwich.

"How about turning on the AC?" he asked.

"Are you serious?"

"Yeah. It's a million degrees in here."

"I'm not going to pollute the atmosphere just so you can be comfortable."

"I can't believe I asked."

TWENTY

Derek Costello at 111 Huntington Terrace still wasn't in. Neither was his next-door neighbor, Ella Didrickson, the woman who had seen Walter and Gwen come home on the day of the murder.

A short, powerfully built man was cutting the grass with a push mower at the house beside the Richardsons'.

"Mr. Thelen?" Sonya asked.

"That's me." He mopped his brow while Sonya told him why she and Matt were there.

"Ray Richardson. Haven't heard that name in a long time." He shook his head sorrowfully. "It was a terrible thing. Just terrible."

"Were you home that day?" Sonya asked.

"No. I was out of town all week. Didn't find out about it until I got back. I knew things between Ray and Walter were coming to a head, but I never thought it would end up the way it did."

"Coming to a head?" Matt asked. "How?"

"They had a big dustup the day before it happened. I was out doing some errands. When I came home, they were in the driveway. Walter was yelling at Ray. You know that Ray was doing drugs, right?" Matt and Sonya nodded. "*You better clean up your act, boy*, Walter was saying. *I'm tired of your crap. You come home wasted one more time, and you're gonna have to find somewhere else to live.*"

"What did Ray do?" Sonya asked.

"He just stood there, smirking like a real smart-ass. Walter lost it. He slapped Ray across the face. Hard. I heard it from here. They stared at each other for a few seconds, not saying anything. Then Ray got this cold look on his face. Told Walter that if he ever laid a hand on him again, he'd kill him."

That wasn't the way Ray had described it, Matt recalled. An argument about his lifestyle was how he had put it. Had he forgotten that he'd threatened to kill his dad, or did he just think it wasn't worth mentioning?

"Why didn't you tell the police?" Matt asked.

"By the time I heard about the murders, Ray had already pled guilty. No point in my getting involved."

"What do you make of that?" Matt asked Sonya when they were back on the sidewalk.

"It doesn't mean anything. Haven't you ever told anybody you wanted to kill them?"

"Yeah, but they didn't end up dead the next day. I know, I know. If Ray was guilty, he wouldn't be dead set on spending the rest of his life in jail." But was it really as simple as that? he wondered. He still didn't see how Walter could have drunk an entire beer without noticing that the back door had been kicked in, no matter how hard he was concentrating on the newspaper. *Nothing about this case makes sense.* He felt like a dog chasing its tail.

A chunky man in a tank top sat on the porch of the house on the corner. His bald head glistened with sweat.

"Martin Porter?" Sonya said after looking at the spreadsheet.

"Sup, Matt," Porter said, rising to his feet. He extended his fist in a pathetic attempt to be cool, smiling broadly when Matt jabbed it with his own. "Marty Porter. I own the travel agency on Deacon Street. We handled the arrangements when you guys went to the capital for the game. The hotel was sweet, wasn't it?"

"It was great."

"Man, you really messed up your leg, didn't you?"

Thanks for pointing that out.

Sonya jumped in. "We're with the Justice Project," she said and then explained why she and Matt were at his door.

"I was home, but I didn't see anything," Porter said.

"Thanks for your time," Matt said.

"I played some ball myself back in the day," Porter said, missing the cue to say goodbye. "Three-year starter at Oakwood. Tight end." A wistful look crossed his face. "Game day. There's nothing like it, is there? Running onto the field, the crowd going crazy, the cheerleaders jumping all over the place." He looked at Sonya as if he expected her to wave a pom-pom. "I still dream about it, believe it or not. Best days of my life."

Matt and Sonya took advantage of his reverie to make their escape.

Best days of my life, Matt repeated to himself as he swayed down the path. Was he going to end up like that? Living in the past, dreaming about what might have been? *Screw that.* Across the street a young couple was staring at him. He glared at them angrily. *And screw you too.*

The next hour was an exercise in frustration. Eleven households visited. Eleven households where nobody had seen a thing.

"I'm beat," Sonya said when they were done.

"It's only two thirty. Plenty of time for another circuit."

"If I wasn't so tired, I'd call your bluff."

They were walking to Sonya's car when a blue Toyota pulled into the driveway of number 111. A scrawny man with a goatee got out of the car.

"Mr. Costello?" Sonya asked.

"If you're with the Jehovah's Witnesses, I'm not interested."

"It's nothing like that, sir," Sonya assured him before explaining why she and Matt were there.

"Were you home that day?" Matt asked.

"I was here when Walter came back from work."

"Do you remember what time that was?"

"Just after three."

"Are you sure?" Sonya asked.

"Positive. I was working the morning shift at the cement plant in Hayward." He waved his hand in the general direction of Hayward, a small town a few miles north of Snowden. "I got home at three and saw Walter pulling into the driveway."

"Do you know Ella Didrickson?"

Costello smiled. "Sure. I know Ella. She's the neighborhood watch all by herself."

"She told the police she saw Walter come home at four."

Costello was unfazed by the apparent discrepancy. "I went outside fifteen minutes or so after I got home. I was going to a friend's house to watch a ball game. Walter was driving away. Ella must have seen him when he came back." He shrugged. "I blame the drugs. Ray was a nice kid until he started messing around with that stuff."

"There's your explanation for the beer," Sonya said after they left the Costello residence. "Walter drank it when he came home at three. The burglar broke in after he left the house at three fifteen, and he was still there when Walter got back at four."

Makes sense, Matt thought. He could stop chasing his tail. But they were no closer to proving Ray was innocent than they were the day they started.

TWENTY-ONE

Matt sliced through the water, pulling with all his strength until he reached the end of the pool. He grabbed the ledge, glancing at his watch as he caught his breath. Forty lengths in a shade under thirty-five minutes wouldn't get him into the Olympics, but it wasn't bad, considering he'd only been able to do eight when he started swimming ten days earlier.

"Looking good," the lifeguard said. "We'll make a swimmer out of you yet."

"You've got to teach me how to do a flip turn."

"I'll show you tomorrow. It's easy."

"I'll be here."

Matt pulled himself out of the pool. He'd forgotten how good it felt to push his body to the limit, the pleasure he got from feeling the fatigue in his muscles. And he enjoyed swimming more than he had predicted. He liked the feeling of being in a world of his own, where nothing existed except him and the water, where nobody could see that there was something wrong with him. Where he felt like he was normal.

★ ★ ★

"Thank you very much, Mr. Donaldson," Matt said into the phone. "I'll call you next week to arrange the pickup." He added the information to his list of donations for the silent auction: *Donaldson Electronics. 42" flat-screen* TV.

"Don't forget to come by and sign my championship-game program," Donaldson said.

"I'll drop into the store next chance I get."

Matt had known Donaldson was going to make a donation as soon as he introduced himself. Like just about everybody else on Matt's list, Donaldson was more interested in talking about football than in hearing about the work the Justice Project was doing. And after chewing Matt's ear off for ten minutes, he could hardly refuse to participate in the auction. It was no accident Jesse had given Matt the task of soliciting donations.

So far he had obtained enough household goods to furnish a mansion, dozens of gift certificates and an all-expenses-paid trip for two to New York City, the last donated by the Porter Travel Agency after Matt buttered up Marty Porter by faking a burning desire to hear all about his glory days at Oakland High.

The Snowden Vision Center had just come through with a year's supply of contact lenses when Mayor Jamie Jenkins came into the office, wearing a matching skirt and jacket. She and Angela exchanged kisses.

"What a pleasant surprise," Angela said.

"I have a meeting across the street and thought I'd drop in and say hello."

"Jesse will be sorry he missed you. Thanks so much for offering to host the cocktail party. We really appreciate it."

"It's the least we can do," Jamie replied. "Hello, Matt. Nice to see you again."

"You too," Matt said.

"I was at a mayors' convention in the capital last month, and I can't tell you how many people congratulated me on the victory. You and your teammates put this town on the map."

"Thanks."

"This is our other summer intern, Sonya Livingstone," Angela said.

"Dan told me you were working here. Please say hello to your father for me."

"I will," Sonya said.

"Dan mentioned you were looking into Ray Richardson's case," Jamie said to Angela.

"Only unofficially," Angela said, in case the mayor shared her father's misgivings.

"I think that's great," Jamie assured her. "I was blown away when Dan told me that Ray refuses to ask for parole. Unbelievable."

"Did you know Ray?" Sonya asked.

"Just to say hello. We were in the same English class when we were juniors, but midway through the year my father sent me to an all-girls school. He thought being around boys was distracting me from my studies."

Didn't keep her away from Dan Burke, Matt thought.

"I knew Walter well," Jamie added, turning serious. "He was a wonderful man. I was devastated when I found out he'd been killed. He was very kind to me. Very kind." Her voice cracked with emotion. "After Ray pled guilty it never crossed my mind that he might be innocent. Have you come up with anything?"

"Not yet," Sonya said, her tone reflecting an optimism Matt saw no reason to share.

He and Sonya had been back to the Richardsons' neighborhood twice in the week and a half since they first went there, and they had spoken to dozens of former residents who had moved away. But all they had learned was that Ray was a sweet kid until he started doing drugs and that Matt's accident was the Snowden equivalent of the sinking of the *Titanic*. Meanwhile, the number of potential witnesses had dwindled to thirty-seven.

"I better run," Jamie said. "Good luck with the case. And the next time you see Ray, please tell him what a fine man his father was."

"If my daughter was acting out, an all-girls school is the last place I'd send her," Sonya said after Jamie left. "I have a friend whose dad sent her to St. Andrews. You wouldn't believe the stories she told me about some of the girls."

"Do you have names and contact info?" Matt asked.

"He's a funny guy," Angela said.

"A riot," Sonya agreed.

★ ★ ★

Matt stayed on at the end of the day to make a few more phone calls. He had just cajoled one of his former teammates, Andy Evelyn, whose dad owned the Snowden Limousine Service, into donating a limo and driver for New Year's Eve when Anthony Blanchard called.

"Sup, AB? How's life on the coast?"

"Not good. I'm playing like shit. I'm dropping balls I could have caught in junior high. You wouldn't believe how big and fast everybody is. I feel like I'm in over my head."

"You've only been out there for a couple of weeks, man. Give it some time. If you didn't belong, they wouldn't have given you a scholarship."

Matt felt for his friend, but it was weird to be commiserating with Anthony over an opportunity he'd been robbed of. His English teacher would call it ironic.

"I'm sorry, man," Anthony said. "Here I am whining about myself, and look what you've got to deal with. How are you doing?"

"Hanging in there."

"Have you seen any of the guys?"

"You asking if I'm getting out of the apartment?"

"Your words. Not mine."

"I've seen The Goon a few times. He wants to be called Allan from now on. Says Goon isn't dignified."

"That ain't going to happen."

"That's what I told him."

They talked for a few more minutes, until it was time for Anthony to go to practice.

"I'll see you next week at graduation," Anthony said. "Be strong, brother."

"I'm trying."

Matt was about to call it a day when a courier arrived with an envelope from Ralph Chadwick, the Justice Project's investigator. It contained the Richardsons' phone records from the day of the murder. Only two calls had been made that day. The first was at 3:07 PM, a few minutes after Derek Costello saw Walter arrive at the house, and the second was at 3:13.

Matt called the first number.

"Dan Burke's office," a woman said pleasantly.

Matt hung up. That fits, he thought. Burke had said Walter called him after he picked up the replacement car from the limo company, wanting to know if the mayor needed him.

He dialed the second number. "Violet Bailey and Associates," a voice chirped.

Matt was about to hang up when he remembered that Ray's mother, Gwen, had worked for Violet Bailey. Walter must have been calling her. It was hard to imagine that Violet would remember anything after all these years, but it was worth a shot.

To Matt's surprise, Violet remembered the phone call. "I don't know what Walter said to Gwen, but she was upset when she got off the phone. *The shit's going to hit the fan,* she told me. Those were her exact words."

"Do you know what she meant?"

"No idea. I asked, but she didn't want to talk about it."

Matt locked up and went outside.

The shit is going to hit the fan. Gwen's words nagged at him all the way home. What had Walter told Gwen?

TWENTY-TWO

Sonya was already at the office when Matt arrived at 7:30 the next morning. The crime scene photos were laid out on her desk.

It had been her idea to come in early and go over the file again. "We must have missed something," she had said the night before when Matt told her about Gwen's comment to Violet Bailey.

Matt had his doubts. He and Sonya had been through the file so many times that they knew it by heart. But they owed it to Ray to go through it again. Learning how to do a flip turn would have to wait.

Sonya tapped on the photo of the black sedan in the garage. "Let's start with what we know. At three o'clock Derek Costello sees Walter drive the replacement car from the limo company into the garage."

"He had to get out of the car to open the garage door," Matt said. "He wouldn't have done that if he knew he was going to be leaving in a few minutes. He would have parked in the driveway and gone in through the front door."

"I agree. Walter comes into the kitchen from the garage, opens a beer, sits down at the kitchen table and starts reading the newspaper." She pointed at the photo showing the *Sunday Sentinel* on the kitchen table beside the bottle of beer and the chauffeur's hat. "At 3:07 he calls Dan Burke, who tells him the mayor doesn't need him. At 3:13 he calls Gwen, who gets off the phone and tells Violet that *the shit is going to hit the fan.* He must have seen something between the time he got to the house and the time he called Gwen. But what?"

"Maybe it was something in the newspaper," Matt suggested. He peered at the photo, but he could only make out the headline: *Snowden Woman Killed in Hit-and-Run. Police Looking for Black Sedan.* "Are the *Sentinel's* back issues online?"

Sonya navigated to the newspaper's website and found the issue from the day of the murders. "Check this out," she said. Midway down the front page was a photo of the Chief— far younger than the old man they'd met—in a restaurant booth with an attractive young blonde. The headline of the story read *Chief Promises Help for Single Mothers.* "Doug Cunningham said the Chief was playing around. Makes you wonder what kind of help he was offering her."

"Probably the same type of help he offered my mom," Matt said. He told Sonya what his dad had told him.

"Gross." She clicked on the link to page two.

Matt glanced at the *Sentinel* headline again. *Snowden Woman Killed in Hit-and-Run. Police Looking for Black Sedan.*

A black sedan.

"Go back to the front page again," he said. "The article about the hit-and-run."

> A West Side woman has died following a hit-and-run early this morning on Amsterdam Avenue. Anita Sonnenberg, 52, was rushed to hospital by ambulance but was pronounced dead on arrival. An eyewitness said the victim was crossing the street when she was struck by a late-model black sedan that fled the scene without stopping. The witness did not see the driver but said a young female was sitting in the passenger seat. Anyone with information is asked to call Snowden Police at 806-9317.

"Holy shit," Matt said.

"I don't get it," Sonya said.

"The Chief's car was a black sedan. The day after the hit-and-run, Walter took it in for repairs. And we know the Chief liked to fool around. The young woman in the car could have been one of his girlfriends."

"You think the Chief was driving? Are you insane?"

"Something happened to the car, or Walter wouldn't have had to take it in," Matt pointed out. "And remember how the Chief tried to stop us from investigating Ray's case with that bullshit about us misusing Justice Project resources? What if Walter read the article and figured out that the Chief was responsible for the hit-and-run? Then he calls Gwen and tells her. That would explain the *shit's going to hit the fan* comment."

"Are you saying the Chief killed Walter?"

"He couldn't let anyone know about the hit-and-run. He would have gone to jail."

"How did the Chief find out that Walter knew about it?"

"Walter told him. That's where he went when he left the house at 3:15. To see the Chief."

"Wouldn't he have gone to the police?"

"Not without speaking to the Chief first."

"But Walter wasn't killed at Lawson House," Sonya pointed out. "He was killed in his own house."

"The Chief couldn't kill him at Lawson House. What would he do with the body? He must have persuaded Walter to take him back to his house. The limo's windows are tinted, so nobody would have seen that the Chief was in the car. They go into the kitchen from the garage. The Chief kills Walter, but before he can leave, Gwen comes home, so he has to kill her too. Then he fakes the burglary so the police will think a robber did it."

"Wait a minute," Sonya said. "Just because Walter took the car in for repairs doesn't mean it was in an accident. For all we know, the car could have been keyed by an angry husband."

Matt chuckled. He looked at the photo of the black sedan. The limo company's name was on the license plate. Snowden Limousine Service. He reached for his phone.

"Put it on speaker," Sonya said.

"Snowden Limousine Service. Andy Evelyn speaking," a teenage voice squeaked.

"Hey, Andy. It's Matt."

"I hope you're not going to hit me up for something else for the auction. My dad chewed me out for giving you the car and driver."

"It's not about that."

Matt and Sonya waited impatiently while Andy dug out the paperwork.

"What was the problem with the car?" Matt asked when Andy was back on the phone.

"I don't know. All it says on the invoice is *Repairs. $1,965*."

"Is there any way of finding out what they did?"

"The body shop would have had a work order, but I don't know if they would have kept it all this time."

Matt and Sonya exchanged a hopeful look. A body shop. That's where Walter would have taken the car if it had been in an accident. "What's the name of the place?" Matt asked.

"Bob's Auto Body on Crawford. We don't use them anymore. The new owner's a real bitch."

"He would never say that about a man," Sonya said after Andy hung up. "A man who's tough is just tough. But when a woman's tough, she's a bitch."

Matt nodded. He wasn't going to touch that one with a ten-foot pole.

TWENTY-THREE

"I didn't know there were so many bad drivers in Snowden," Matt joked when they got to Bob's Body Shop at the end of the day. Cars were raised on hoists in each of the three bays, tended to by workers in greasy overalls, and another six cars with varying degrees of damage were parked in front.

A woman behind a cluttered desk in a small office was on the phone, the name Madge stitched on her shirt.

"We can't look at your car until Friday morning," Madge barked into the phone. "Bring it in then." She tossed her phone on the desk and looked up at Matt and Sonya.

"We're with the Justice Project," Matt told her. "We're looking for some information about one of our cases."

"Do I look like I have time to go on a scavenger hunt?"

"I can see you're really busy," Matt said, flashing a smile. "But it's really important."

"I know who you are. You're that football player."

"Guilty." This is going to be easy, he thought.

"My ex-husband played football. It was all he ever talked about. Biggest jackass I ever met. Now get lost." The phone rang. Madge picked it up. "Bob's Auto Body. Just a minute." She put the phone down and walked out to the garage. Sonya nudged Matt and pointed to a shelf above the window that held dusty binders labeled by year.

"When's the Camry going to be ready?" Madge yelled.

"Not today," a voice shouted back.

"Why are you still here?" she said to Matt and Sonya when she returned. She picked up the phone. "Call back tomorrow."

Sonya moved to the far side of Madge's desk. "I don't feel so good," she said. She covered her mouth and leaned over the desk as if she was going to throw up.

Madge picked up the wastepaper basket and held it out in front of Sonya, her back to Matt. "Use this," she ordered.

Matt quickly grabbed the binder they needed and shoved it into his backpack. He rushed to Sonya's side. "Are you okay?" he asked.

"False alarm," Sonya said, straightening up. "Mom said the first three months are the worst." Madge looked at her openmouthed. "We should go," Sonya said to Matt. "I need to lie down."

Matt put his arm around her shoulder and helped her out the door. "I told you to use a condom," Sonya said angrily, in a voice loud enough for Madge to hear.

"We've been through that," Matt said, pretending to be just as angry. "Matt Junior needs a sibling."

They were howling with laughter by the time they got to Sonya's car.

"Your friend at the limo company was right," Sonya said. "That woman *is* a bitch."

Matt opened the binder. It didn't take long to find the work order he was looking for. *Lincoln Continental. License: THE CHIEF. Replace hood and front bumper.*

"Oh my god," Sonya said. They stared at each other wordlessly. Then Sonya called Jesse and left him a message to call her back.

"It could be a coincidence," Matt suggested.

Sonya gave him a look that said she didn't believe that any more than he did. "That was really smart, the way you figured out that the Chief's car was involved in the hit-and-run."

"Not bad for a Neanderthal who needs to take off his shoes and socks to count past ten," Matt joked.

"That really pissed you off, didn't it?"

"Not as much as our showing up barefoot did you."

"That was cute. I'll give you that. Was that your idea?"

Matt nodded. "Did you actually think your petition would change anything?"

"No. Not in Snowden, where even God wears the green-and-gold."

"So why did you do it? You don't even play sports."

"Because it was the right thing to do. Why shouldn't women athletes get the same support men do?"

★ ★ ★

Sonya dropped Matt off in front of his apartment. "I'll call you as soon as I hear from Jesse."

An envelope from Eastern State was in the mailbox. Matt opened it when he got into the apartment. Inside was a letter congratulating him on being accepted into the school, along with the course curriculum.

Congratulations! What a joke. If you could walk and chew gum at the same time, you were pretty much guaranteed acceptance to Eastern State. He thumbed through the course curriculum, but nothing registered with him. He was too busy trying to process what he and Sonya had discovered.

Had the Chief really killed Walter and Gwen? He and Sonya had been so sure of it, but here in his living room, in the hard light of day, it seemed preposterous. He went over the facts again and again, and each time he reached the same conclusion. The Chief was guilty. It gave Matt goose bumps to think that Ray's nightmare was coming to an end, that he would soon be walking out of prison a free man.

He stared at his phone, commanding it to ring. An hour passed before it obeyed.

"What did Jesse say?" he asked Sonya anxiously.

"Do you have your computer?"

"Yeah. Why?"

"Go to the *Sentinel*'s website and find the paper from the day of the murder."

"Got it," he said, when it was up on his screen.

"Read the last paragraph of the article, about the mayor's meeting in the restaurant with the blonde."

Matt read it out loud. "*'I intend to work with City Council to make sure single mothers get the help they deserve,' the Chief said in an interview at Snowden Airport Saturday afternoon, minutes before he boarded a plane to Chicago to attend a charity dinner.'"*

Minutes before he boarded a plane. It took a moment for Matt to grasp the implication. The Chief had been in Chicago at the time of the hit-and-run. He had nothing to do with the murders.

Matt and Sonya were back at square one.

TWENTY-FOUR

Matt had just come through the door to the office when Anthony texted him.

On my way to the airport. See you at graduation tomorrow.

Matt texted a reply. **CU then.**

"Do you want to go to Cooley Park after work?" Sonya asked after Matt got himself a coffee. "It won't take long. We only have four houses left to visit," she added in a tone of voice that made it clear she didn't hold out much hope that anything would come of it.

Matt was inclined to agree. In the two weeks following the fiasco with the Chief, he and Sonya had devoted every free moment to following up with the people on their list. Only one person they contacted, Leon Patterson, whose mother, Lenore, was Jolene's good friend, had any information about the case, but he didn't tell them anything they didn't already know. Leon sent an email from Brazil saying that he had seen Ray come out the back gate of the Richardsons' house on the afternoon of the murders and head down the alley toward Delaney Heights.

That left only seven names on the list: the four in Cooley Park and three that Ralph Chadwick, the Justice Project's investigator, was looking for because Matt and Sonya had been unable to track them down.

"Today's not good," Matt said. "I'm seeing Emma. How's Saturday?"

"That works."

Matt sat down at his desk. A feeling of sadness washed over him. In two days Emma would be leaving for California to start her job with the theater company. She would be working there until school started in September. Who knew when they would see each other again?

"I know it doesn't seem like it now," Sonya said, "but you'll meet somebody else."

"It won't be the same."

"You know this song?" Sonya began singing, her voice intense. "*I'll always love you. I'll always love you. I'll always love you.*" Her voice dropped to a whisper. "*Until I find somebody new.*"

Matt laughed. "That's not very romantic."

"All I'm saying is, I don't believe people have a soul mate—that there's only one person in the world who we're meant to be with. What if that person lives in another country, somewhere you'll never go to? You'd never meet each other. There are lots of people you can fall in love with."

Matt couldn't argue with the logic, but it didn't make Emma's going away any easier to take.

★ ★ ★

Emma was already in the café when Matt arrived. She was seated at the back, her head in a book. He stood and watched her for a moment. Her face was tanned a deep bronze from her time in the country.

She's so beautiful, Matt thought. He remembered the first time they had had sex. They had been at her parents' place at the lake. They'd been going out for a year by then. They'd talked before about having sex, but Emma had always said she wasn't ready. "I can wait," he had told her. "I don't want you to do anything you don't want to do."

They'd been fooling around on the deck. Emma's mother and father had taken her kid brother, Jake, aka the "little shit," to the fair in Midland. All of a sudden Emma sat up, stared into his eyes and then took him by the hand and led him into her bedroom. He had driven back to town later that afternoon. He had been so excited about finally doing it that he'd run a red light and almost gotten into a car accident.

Emma looked up from her book as he swayed toward her. They hugged. She smelled like flowers, a familiar smell that triggered a jumble of feelings, of desire and of loss.

"Did you have fun at the lake?" he asked.

"The water was freezing, my parents argued the whole time, and the little shit was a little shit."

"Sorry I wasn't there," Matt said. He was only half joking. "How have you been?"

"It's been tough. I'm not going to lie."

Emma covered his hands with hers. For a moment he imagined that she was going to tell him she had decided to stay in Snowden after all. *Get a grip, dude.*

"Let's get out of here," she said.

They left the café and walked to the river. Matt's spirits sank with every awkward step. In the month since he'd shed the crutches, he had learned to accept the looks that came his way without feeling like he was a member of a lesser species. But as he walked beside Emma, he was painfully aware of his ludicrous gait. They were *Beauty and the Beast* come to life.

They sat down on a bench facing the river. Canoeists paddled by, some drifting downstream, others working against the current.

"The hardest thing is knowing that it's never going to end, that I'm going to be like this for the rest of my life," Matt said. "It's my first thought when I wake up, and it's my last thought before I fall asleep. It just never freaking ends."

Emma put her hand on his cheek. That was all it took to open the floodgates. She held him in her arms as he sobbed. "Let it out," she whispered.

He surrendered to the feelings he had kept bottled up inside for so long, his tears releasing his sadness and pain and grief in a way that words never could.

He cried until he was all cried out. He felt spent, depleted, as if he had just gone through a grueling workout. But he also felt lighter, as if he'd shed all the emotional baggage he had been carrying for so long. The black cloud that had hovered over him had lifted. At least for now. It could only have happened with Emma. Even though they were no longer together, he still felt closer to her than to anybody else in the world.

"I am going to miss you," he said. "I'm happy for you, but I'm really going to miss you."

"I'm going to miss you too. But I'm only going to be a phone call away."

"Until those Hollywood producers see you. Then it'll be *Matt who*?"

Emma laughed. "*Matt Barnes*?" she said in a puzzled voice. She shook her head. "*Doesn't ring a bell.*"

Matt laughed. A young couple paddled by. The boy, sitting in the stern, dropped his paddle. He reached for it, almost tipping the canoe, before it steadied.

"Remember our first camping trip?" Emma asked.

"Rained the entire time."

"We ate cold beans for three days."

"Best trip ever."

Time flew by as Matt and Emma reminisced, but eventually Emma had to go.

"Want to walk me home?" she asked.

"I'm going to hang here for a while." They would see each other the next day at graduation, but this was goodbye. There was no point in prolonging the agony.

They hugged fiercely, reluctant to let go, as if time would stand still as long as they were holding each other. This time Emma was the one who started crying. "I'll always love you," she said through her tears when they finally pulled apart.

"I'll always love you too."

He watched Emma walk away and out of his life. The words to Sonya's refrain came back to him. *I'll always love you. I'll always love you...Until I find somebody new.*

The black cloud descended. He didn't want to find anybody new.

TWENTY-FIVE

"I'll see you after the ceremony," Matt's father said the next day before going into the stands where the families of the graduating students were seated.

Matt wished graduation wasn't taking place on the football field. Not that it made much difference—no matter where the event was held, he would still have to hobble across a stage in front of all these people. The fact that he would have to do it here, on the site of his former triumphs, was just one more bitter irony in a life full of bitter ironies.

Steve Kowalski and a few other teammates, all wearing caps and gowns, stood by one of the goalposts. Matt joined them. "They tell us individuality is the key to success, and then they make everybody dress like this," he joked.

"And charge us fifty bucks for the privilege," Steve said.

"They should have charged you a hundred," Matt said. "There's enough material there to clothe a village."

Steve was searching for a comeback when The Goon joined them. "Gentlemen."

"Goon," everyone yelled in unison, mocking his desire to shed his undignified nickname.

The Goon amiably gave them the finger. "Hard to believe this is the last time we're all going to be on the field together," he said, turning serious. "I don't know what I'm going to do without you guys." The others murmured in agreement. "I know I'll get over it in time, but those first ten minutes are going to be brutal." Everybody laughed.

Matt spotted Emma talking to Rona. He was about to walk toward them when Coach Bennett came up to him, wearing a powder-blue cap and gown from his alma mater, the University of North Carolina.

"Can you come by the office tomorrow?" the coach asked. "There's something I want to discuss with you."

"Sure."

Matt was wondering what the coach wanted, when Anthony Blanchard tapped him on the shoulder.

"Man, it is good to see you," Anthony said as the two boys hugged.

"You too."

"How's it going in LA?" Matt asked.

"I'm settling in. You were right. I just needed some time."

"That's great, man." Matt was genuinely happy for Anthony, but he felt a twinge of envy as well. *If only.*

An announcement boomed over the PA system. "Would everyone please take their seats."

"Are you coming to The Goon's tonight?" Anthony asked as he and Matt walked toward the folding chairs in front of the stage. The Goon was throwing a party for the team's seniors.

"For sure," Matt said. He met Anthony's eyes to let him know that this time he meant it.

Once everybody was seated, Principal Mosley said a few words of introduction and then called Sonya to the stage to give the valedictory address.

"Congratulations, seniors," she began. If she was nervous, she didn't show it. She kept her speech short, but she hit all the right notes. She recalled her first anxious day as a freshman, recited a few of her favorite memories and mentioned some of the highlights of the past four years, including the state championship—which drew a loud and sustained cheer from the crowd. She even threw in a joke: "Your parents are incredibly proud of you, so today would be a good time to ask them for money." Everyone laughed. "It's been an amazing four years for all of us," she went on. "We've forged friendships that will last a lifetime—or at least through the weekend." That drew another laugh. "But in a very real way our lives are just beginning. So as great as the past four years have been, don't let them be the best of your life."

Was it his imagination, Matt wondered, or was Sonya looking at him?

Principal Mosley stepped up to the podium and began reading out the names of the graduating students in alphabetical order.

"James Allen."

Jimmy bounced up the steps and across the stage. He shook hands with Mosley, who muttered a few words as he handed him his diploma.

Mosley read out the next name. "Allan Baker."

"Goon!" the entire football team shouted. Goon blew them a kiss and then claimed his diploma.

"Matt Barnes."

It was the moment Matt had been dreading. He slowly climbed the stairs. A hush fell over the crowd as he lurched toward the principal. He was halfway there when someone started clapping.

"Clear eyes," Anthony's deep voice boomed out.

The rest of his teammates joined in. "Full hearts. Can't lose."

By the time Matt reached the podium, the entire graduating class was applauding, along with their guests. Everybody was on their feet. A chill ran up Matt's spine.

"Congratulations, Matt," Mosley said, his voice cracking with emotion as he handed Matt his diploma.

The rest of the ceremony passed in a blur. Matt didn't know what to make of what had happened. Was it love or pity?

Probably both, he thought.

TWENTY-SIX

Jesse was outside the office, munching on a chocolate bar, when Matt arrived the next day. He held out the bar to Matt.

"Sorry I'm late," Matt said, suppressing a yawn as he took a square. The Goon's party had lasted until four in the morning. Everybody knew it was the last time they would be together as a group, and nobody had wanted it to end.

"You only graduate once," Jesse said. "I heard about what happened at the ceremony yesterday. That must have been something."

"It was weird."

"How so?"

"It isn't like I actually did anything—other than get maimed for life."

"There's a lot more to it than that."

"I know. But nobody would have cheered if I hadn't limped across the stage."

"I know how you feel. When I got out of prison, people treated me like I was a hero. But I hadn't done anything either. I felt like I was being celebrated for being a victim."

Exactly, Matt thought.

"It was like I had a name tag on my shirt that said *Jesse Donovan, Wrongly Convicted*. I bought into it until I realized that just because other people defined me as a victim didn't mean I had to define myself the same way." Jesse smiled. "Sorry for the sermon. Angela says I should have been a preacher."

"That's okay." Matt didn't mind getting a sermon from Jesse. "How long did it take until you threw away the name tag?"

"It took a while."

Matt decided not to ask how long.

"That was a great speech you gave," Matt said to Sonya when he was seated at his desk.

"Thanks. But it was your day."

"I'm glad it's over."

"It was inspiring."

"Yeah, right."

"It inspired me. It gave me the courage to tell my parents I was gay."

"Really?"

"I told them when I got home last night."

"What did they say?"

"My dad said they were wondering when I was going to tell them."

"Parents," Matt said with a mock shake of his head. "Who can understand them?"

Sonya laughed. "They want to meet Morgan."

"I hope that goes better for you than it did for me. After Emma and I had been going out for a few months, her parents invited me to dinner. I was nervous at the start, but they were really friendly. Everything's going great. Then, while we're having dessert—I'm sitting across the table from Emma and her dad—I decide, for some insane reason, that it would be a good idea to play footsie with her. I start rubbing my foot against her leg. At least, I think it's her leg—until she gets up and goes to the washroom."

Sonya erupted in laughter. "You're kidding."

"Nope. Her dad looked at me and said, *I really like you too, Matt.*"

Sonya laughed again. "I'll tell Morgan to keep her feet on the floor."

★ ★ ★

"Take a seat," Coach Bennett said, gesturing to a chair when Matt arrived at his office. "That was something else yesterday. Brought a tear to my eye, I don't mind telling you." He took a swig of his coffee. "I'll get right to the point. How would you like to work with the team next year as our quarterback coach? I've got some money in the budget—not a lot, but we'd be able to pay you a couple thousand dollars. We'd have to work around your class schedule, of course, but that shouldn't be a problem."

Matt didn't know what to say. The money would come in handy, but he didn't know if he could stand being on a football field, watching other people do what he no longer could.

"I'm thinking of putting in the wishbone offense," Coach Bennett continued. "It would take advantage of Damon's athleticism," he said, referring to the previous year's backup quarterback, who would be stepping into the starting role. He looked at Matt. "You don't have to decide now. We don't start practice until the middle of August. Think it over, and get back to me."

Matt walked down the deserted hallway. Coach Bennett's offer reminded him of an episode of *Friday Night Lights*. The team's all-star quarterback, Jason Street, had ended up in a wheelchair, paralyzed from the waist down, after a nasty hit on the football field. When his coach offered him a job as quarterback coach, he jumped at the offer. And he'd had it a lot worse than Matt did.

But that was a TV show. This was his life.

He stopped in front of the mural of the team's victory parade. A familiar sadness settled over him, but a moment later it was replaced by anger. Anger at himself. Was he going to just lie down in a corner and whimper for the rest of his life because there weren't going to be any more parades? *Screw that.*

He walked back to the coach's office. Too bad he didn't know anything about the wishbone offense, he thought, but fortunately there was someone at home who did.

TWENTY-SEVEN

The little boy with the Mohawk haircut was running through a sprinkler on the lawn of the Richardsons' former house when Matt and Sonya arrived Saturday morning. The heat assaulted Matt as soon as he got out of the car. It was going to be another scorcher. He was glad they only had four houses to visit.

Nobody at the first three houses had any helpful information. No surprise there, Matt thought. That left Ella Didrickson, the woman who had seen Walter and Gwen on the day they were killed. As they walked up the front path, Matt saw a wrinkled old face peering out at them from a window.

Sonya knocked. The door opened a few inches. It was secured by a chain. The wrinkled face stared out at them.

"Who did you say you worked for?" Ella Didrickson asked after Sonya explained why she and Matt were there.

"The Justice Project."

"Do you have ID?"

Sonya held out her business card. A liver-spotted hand snatched it. A minute later Ella unlatched the door and led them into the living room.

"Please sit down." She pointed to a couch covered in plastic.

Ella confirmed what she had told the police. Walter arrived around four, and Gwen drove up fifteen minutes later. She didn't have anything else to add.

"Were you outside when Walter arrived?" Sonya asked as they got up to leave.

"Why do you ask?"

Matt wondered the same thing.

"I notice that you can't see the Richardsons' house from here."

Matt looked outside. He could see the house across the street and a couple of others farther down, but the Richardson house was out of his line of sight.

"I was at the window," Ella explained. "There had been several break-ins in the neighborhood, and I was keeping an eye out for anyone who looked suspicious."

Matt smiled to himself as he recalled what Derek Costello had said about her. *She's the neighborhood watch all by herself.*

"I guess that's it," Matt said dejectedly when they got to the car.

"Maybe Ralph Chadwick will come up with something," Sonya said, but she didn't sound very optimistic.

"Let's hope, because I really don't want to have to tell Jolene there's nothing we can do."

As they drove away he spotted Ella back at her post by the window.

"What are you doing tonight?" Sonya asked when they arrived at Matt's apartment building.

"Nothing. Dinner with my dad."

"*The Thin Blue Line* is playing at the Fox. It's a documentary about a guy who was wrongfully convicted of killing a police officer. We should go."

"Sounds good."

Life is strange, Matt thought as Sonya drove off. If anybody had told him a month ago that he and Sonya would be friends, he'd have said they were crazy.

His dad was hooking up his computer to the TV when Matt walked in. "How's it going, Coach?" his father asked.

Matt's dad had been thrilled when Matt announced that he was the Falcons' new quarterback coach. And his mother, who had made her weekly call from Saudi Arabia the night before, had been over the moon. "That's fantastic. Really fantastic," she had said. She couldn't have been more enthusiastic if he'd been elected president. She obviously felt this was some kind of turning point—and maybe it was.

"I downloaded some Oklahoma game tapes from the nineties," Matt's father said. "Nobody ran the wishbone better than they did," he added, referring to Coach Bennett's new offense. "The key was their quarterback, Jamelle Holieway.

In the wishbone, the quarterback has to make a split-second decision on every play, and Holieway was a master at it."

It didn't take long for Matt to see that his father was right. Jamelle Holieway was amazing. You never knew what he was going to do with the ball until the last second. "Cool as a cucumber," his dad said after a particularly outstanding play.

The next hour flew by, triggering memories of all the times Matt and his father had studied game tape of the Falcons' opponents. But the memories were bittersweet. As much as he enjoyed sharing his passion for football with his dad, it was painful knowing that they weren't preparing for one of his own games.

"I know it's not the same, but I never thought we'd be doing this again," his dad said quietly when the game was over. He put a comforting hand on Matt's shoulder. "I have to go see a client. I'll be back for dinner. Don't forget to take out the trash."

"Okay."

Matt glanced at the trophy cabinet after his dad left. It looked bare without the MVP award. No, he thought, it's not the same. Not even close.

He hit the Play button and watched the game again, this time taking notes. Matt was as impressed with Jamelle Holieway as he had been the first time around. He really was as cool as a cucumber.

Matt finished watching the game and then took the trash outside and threw it into the bin in front of the apartment building. He waved at a neighbor across the street whose dog was doing his business against a sign that read *This Is a Neighborhood Watch Community.*

Matt was on his way upstairs when the thought struck him. Ella Didrickson said there had been a lot of burglaries in the neighborhood at the time of the murders. Was it possible they had been committed by the same person who'd broken into Gwen and Walter's house?

Matt navigated to the *Sentinel's* website to see what had been written about the other burglaries, but the site was temporarily down for a server upgrade. He called Sonya.

"I was just about to text you," she said. "The film starts at seven."

"Change of plans."

★ ★ ★

Twenty-five minutes later they were at the front desk of the Snowden Public Library. "The back issues of the *Sentinel* are on microfilm," the librarian said. "Give me a few minutes, and I'll bring you the ones you want."

Matt took a seat in front of one of the microfilm readers while Sonya went to the washroom. A few minutes later the librarian returned with a cardboard box.

"Here you go," she said. "Do you know how to use the reader?"

Matt nodded.

"Great. Bring the box back to the desk when you're done."

Matt opened the box. Inside were a bunch of smaller boxes, one for each week's newspapers. Matt took the one labeled March 28–April 4, removed the spool, threaded the film into the reader, and scrolled through it until the Wednesday, March 31 issue was on the screen in front of him.

RICHARDSON PLEADS GUILTY the headline screamed above a picture of Ray being led out of the courthouse in handcuffs. *Son of Mayor's Driver Sentenced to Life in Prison.* Ray looked like a thirteen-year-old kid.

The case had made the headlines the previous two days as well. Tuesday's offering: *Son of Mayor's Driver Charged with Brutal Murders.* Monday's lead item: *Mayor's Driver and Wife Slain in Home Invasion.*

No wonder Doug Cunningham suspected the Chief had made a deal to keep his name out of the headlines, Matt thought. He was going through the paper for Sunday, the day of the murders, when Sonya rejoined him. She sat down at the reader beside him.

"You can start with this one," Matt said, handing her the box for the previous week.

The *Sentinel* concentrated on local news, so it didn't take Matt long to go through each issue. He was skimming through the March 18 edition—a drunken snowplow operator, ribbon-cutting ceremonies at a day care, and the sighting of a flock of Canada geese—when Sonya gasped. "Oh my god."

Matt got up and peered over Sonya's shoulder. An article dated March 14—two weeks before the murders—was on the screen.

COOLEY PARK HOME INVASION VICTIM IN HOSPITAL AFTER STABBING

Snowden police are searching for a suspect after a Cooley Park man was stabbed yesterday afternoon. Fifty-seven-year-old Edgar Willows is in serious but stable condition at Snowden General Hospital. Mr. Willows told police he was attacked when he came home from work. He was unable to provide a description of his assailant.

It's the third home invasion in Cooley Park in as many weeks. Police believe the same person is responsible for all three crimes. "The break-ins were similar in nature," Police Chief Norm Crosby said. "This suggests they were committed by the same person." Chief Crosby refused to elaborate for fear of jeopardizing the investigation.

Mayor Edward Jenkins has promised to put additional police officers in the area until the perpetrator has been apprehended. "Chief Crosby has briefed me on these robberies," the mayor said. "I will be recommending that

council grant the funds necessary to comply
with his request."

Residents are advised to keep their doors
and windows locked at all times.

Matt and Sonya looked at each other, disbelief giving
way to excitement. Had they just found the key to getting
Ray out of jail?

TWENTY-EIGHT

"There might be something here," Jesse said Monday morning when Matt and Sonya showed him the article in the *Sentinel*. "But let's not get ahead of ourselves. There would have to have been something unusual about those three burglaries to make the police think they were all committed by the same person, and there's nothing about the break-in at the Richardsons' that strikes me as out of the ordinary. Somebody kicked in the back door and grabbed things that would be easy to sell. Your standard break-and-enter.

"We need to find out if anything about these break-ins connects them to the one at the Richardsons'. I have a friend in the police department. I'll give him a call and see if we can get a look at the case reports."

Matt tried to concentrate on his work, but his ears perked up every time the phone rang. The call finally came in just before noon.

"Detective Charney has the files. He'll meet you at the front desk," Jesse announced when he hung up.

Matt and Sonya jumped to their feet. Fifteen minutes later they stepped into the new headquarters of the Snowden Police Department, a modern two-story building across from city hall. Several workmen in overalls were bustling around, in the midst of what was obviously a major renovation.

Detective Charney was a burly man with a thick mustache and a gruff, no-nonsense manner. "This was supposed to be finished a month ago," he growled as he sidestepped two workers carrying a ladder. He ushered Matt and Sonya into an unused office on the main floor and handed Matt three dusty file folders, each labeled with the date and address of the break-in.

"It took me a while to dig these out of storage," he said. "We just moved all the old files over here from the Dungeon"—that was the local nickname for the ancient stone building that had previously housed the police department— "and they haven't been organized yet."

"Do you know why the police thought these three break-ins were committed by the same person?" Matt asked.

Charney shook his head. "Before my time."

"Can we make copies?" Sonya asked.

"Absolutely not," he said firmly. "I shouldn't even be showing these to you. I'm only doing it as a favor to Jesse. You can make notes, but no copies. Bring them back to me when you're done. I'm in the office across the hall."

Matt handed a file to Sonya and took one for himself. His was about a break-in on February 28—a month before the murders—that had taken place three blocks south of the Richardsons' house. According to the police report, Al and Evelyn Wells discovered the break-in when they came home from a shopping trip. The thief had entered through a window at the rear of their house. Evelyn's jewelry was stolen, along with the sterling silver cutlery she had inherited from her mother.

A break-in at the back of the house. The theft of items easy to carry and easy to sell. Your standard break-and-enter, as Jesse would have said.

Matt moved on to the next report. As soon as he read it, his heart started racing.

On the night of the robbery, Evelyn Wells had called the police and told them that when she was cleaning up the kitchen, she discovered a bottle of beer that neither she nor Al had drunk. She said the robber must have left it behind.

Matt leafed through the crime-scene photos until he found one of the kitchen. The sink and counters were full of unwashed dishes. And sitting in the middle of all those dirty dishes was a bottle of Rolling Rock beer. *Oh my god!* Matt's heart kicked into overdrive. *It can't be a coincidence.*

"You're not going to believe this," Sonya said. She looked up from the file she was reading.

"Let me guess. The robber left behind a bottle of Rolling Rock."

"You too?" she asked, incredulous.

Matt nodded. He opened the third file. This time the Rolling Rock was in the living room, on a side table beside a couch in front of the TV. He passed the photo to Sonya.

Matt and Sonya exchanged astonished looks. The man who'd committed these burglaries had killed Walter and Gwen. There could be no doubt.

"We have to find out who this guy is," Sonya said.

"How are we going to do that?"

"Maybe…" Sonya hesitated.

"Maybe what?"

"These break-ins happened before Walter and Gwen were murdered. Maybe he broke into other houses afterward."

"And maybe he got caught," Matt said, completing her thought.

"Let's go see Charney."

"We should make notes before we give the files back."

"Or we could just do this." Sonya took her cell phone out of her purse, turned on her camera and positioned it over a page from the file.

"Charney said we couldn't make copies."

"You must have misunderstood."

"I guess I did," Matt said.

He stood watch by the door while Sonya snapped away.

TWENTY-NINE

"Where are the rest of the files stored?" Sonya asked Detective Charney after she had returned the ones he'd given them.

"In the basement. Why?" He put the returned files in a dented cardboard storage box.

"We want to take a look at them to see if—"

"You can't go through our files." Charney snorted as if he'd never heard anything so ridiculous. "Not without a court order." He looked pointedly at the door.

"How long does it take to get a court order?" Matt asked Sonya as they walked away. He had to speak loudly to make himself heard over the whine of an electric drill.

"It doesn't matter. Jesse will never go for it," Sonya said dejectedly. "He has to keep Ray's case off the books until the Justice Project takes it on officially. Remember?"

It was a total bummer. The evidence they'd discovered was compelling, more than compelling, but the Justice Project wouldn't have the money to take on new cases until after the fundraiser, and with so many cases on the waiting list there was no guarantee Ray's would make the cut. It can't end like this, Matt thought. It just can't.

He stopped in front of the staircase that led to the basement.

"Tell me you're not thinking what I think you're thinking," Sonya said. Matt grinned. "This is insane," she said. Matt grinned again.

They made sure nobody was paying attention to them and then hurried down the stairs into a deserted corridor lined with unpainted drywall. Paint cans were stacked on the concrete floor. A number of rooms led off the corridor. Sonya opened the door to the first room. It was the janitor's supply closet. Matt was about to try the door to the next room when footsteps clomped down the staircase toward them. Sonya raced back to the supply closet. She held the door open for Matt, who hurried in after her.

The door swung shut. They held their breath. The footsteps approached, then stopped.

"How many cans do we need?" a man asked.

"Two eggshell and two semigloss."

Moments later the footsteps receded up the stairs. Matt exhaled in relief.

"Put this on." Sonya handed Matt a pair of blue coveralls and took a pair for herself. After they put them on, Sonya handed Matt a broom, filled a bucket with water and grabbed a mop.

There were six more rooms to check out, but they were all locked. Matt and Sonya were standing at the end of the hallway, wondering what to do next, when footsteps again sounded on the stairs. A cop was coming their way, carrying the dented cardboard box with the burglary files. Matt started sweeping the floor, while Sonya mopped behind him. They kept their heads down.

"Afternoon," the cop said as he passed by.

"Afternoon," Matt responded, without looking up. The cop unlocked the door at the end of the corridor and stepped inside. The door slowly closed behind him.

A moment later the cop came out of the room empty handed and headed for the stairs. The door started to swing shut. At the last second Matt stuck the handle of his broom between the door and the frame.

The cop didn't break stride. As soon as he disappeared from sight, Matt and Sonya hurried into the storage room. Matt turned on the light. Charney hadn't been joking. The room was a mess. Dozens of identical cardboard boxes were piled haphazardly on the floor.

"Is this trespassing?" Matt asked. Trespassing was a misdemeanor, a minor crime, he recalled from law class. The worst that could happen was they'd get fined.

"It's not trespassing," Sonya said. "It's breaking and entering."

That was a felony, a serious crime. Matt tried not to think about what the punishment for that was.

It took twenty minutes to find the boxes for the year in which the Richardsons were murdered. Matt took the box for April. Sonya started with May.

It was slow going. Two hours later Matt was halfway through the October files and ready to give up. If the Richardsons' killer hadn't broken into a house in the seven months after the murders, he had either moved away, chosen another line of work or decided not to push his luck.

"Bingo," Sonya said suddenly, slapping down a photo. It showed a bottle of Rolling Rock on a kitchen counter. A second photo followed a moment later—a mug shot of a man with a shaved head and a cross earring. "His name's Harold Holt. He broke into a house on Brunswick Court in November. The police caught him just as he was leaving."

Matt's body tingled with excitement, as if he'd just thrown a game-winning touchdown pass.

"We did it. We really did it!" Sonya exclaimed, flinging her arms around Matt.

"Unreal. Unfreaking real."

A key turned in the lock of the door. They froze on the spot. There was nowhere to hide. Matt knew he had the same panicked look on his face that he saw on Sonya's.

A telephone rang in the hallway. A muffled voice answered it. Matt stared fearfully at the door. A second passed. And then another. And another. He crept toward the door and leaned an ear against it. Nothing. He opened the door a crack. The hallway was empty. He gave Sonya the thumbs-up. She took out her phone, quickly photographed the documents in Harold Holt's file and put the file back in the box.

Five minutes later the coveralls and cleaning supplies were back in place, and Matt and Sonya were heading to the front door of the police station.

"I've never been so scared," Sonya said.

"Me neither."

"What are you still doing here?" a gruff voice asked.

Matt turned. Detective Charney glared at him. "U-uh…" Matt stuttered.

"We came back because I thought I'd forgotten my cell phone," Sonya said without missing a beat. "It was in my purse all along." She shook her head, as if amazed she could have been such a ditz.

Charney looked at her skeptically, then shook his head and walked away.

"That was smooth," Matt said when they were outside. "You're going to be a great lawyer."

"You're the one who suspected the first three break-ins might be connected to the murders. That was really smart."

"Yeah, but if you hadn't asked Ella how she was able to see Walter and Gwen arrive, we would never have learned about the break-ins in the first place. And we wouldn't even be on the case if you hadn't persuaded Jesse to let us look into it."

"I was surprised he agreed."

"Are you kidding? He didn't stand a chance against you."

"We make a pretty good team," Sonya said.

"It hurts to say that, doesn't it?"

"Kills."

"Tell me the truth," Matt said after they got into Sonya's car. "Did you really believe we'd prove Ray was innocent?"

"Never doubted it for a minute," she said with a smile. She pulled out of the parking lot and turned left.

"Where are you going? The office is in the other direction."

"We're not going to the office. We're going to Jolene's."

Jolene was eating her lunch when they arrived with the good news. It took a few seconds to sink in, and then twenty-one years of accumulated stress seemed to flow out of her face.

"The beer always bothered me," Jolene said when she regained her equilibrium. "Walter was a wine drinker. He hardly ever drank beer." Then she asked the million-dollar question. "When is Ray getting out of jail?"

THIRTY

Matt executed a flip turn and sprinted to the other end of the pool, pushing himself to the limit. He checked his watch. Forty laps in twenty-one minutes, shattering his previous personal best. He felt like he could swim another forty laps, even though he'd barely slept the night before. He'd been too excited after finding out about Harold Holt, and he was still pumped.

He was toweling off when a gaggle of chattering seven-year-olds wearing Snowden Adventure Camp T-shirts came into the pool, followed by their counselor. It was Caitlyn, the girl he'd wimped out on at the sandwich shop. She was even cuter than he remembered. Her staff T-shirt was knotted at the waist, revealing a flat midriff with a rose tattoo. She led her campers to the side of the pool, where the lifeguard gave them their instructions. A little girl with pigtails tugged at Caitlyn's shirt, demanding that she hold her hand.

After the campers were in the water, Matt slung his towel over his shoulders and swayed across the tiled floor

MICHAEL BETCHERMAN

toward Caitlyn, fighting off the instinct to escape into the locker room. He flashed on an image of the seals he'd seen at Marineland, flopping across the tiled floor after they got out of the water.

"Hey, Matt."

At least she remembers my name. "Hey, Caitlyn. How's camp?"

"Still haven't lost anyone. "

Matt laughed. "I haven't seen you guys here before."

"We'll be coming here every Tuesday from now on. How's it going at the Justice Project?"

"Fantastic. We've been working on the case of this guy who's been in jail for twenty-one years, and yesterday we found evidence that proves he's innocent."

"That's amazing. I'd love to hear about it."

That was all the encouragement he needed. He was about to ask Caitlyn if she wanted to grab a coffee after work when the girl with the pigtails shrieked. "Look at me, Caitlyn. Look at me." She was standing in the shallow end, pulling her arms through the water. "I'm swimming. I'm swimming."

"You're doing great, Ashley," Caitlyn said. "Now put your head underwater and blow bubbles like I showed you last time."

Ashley lowered her head toward the water. She got it to within six inches and then started crying inconsolably.

"I haven't lost anybody, but I might drown this one," Caitlyn jokingly whispered as she slipped into the water.

Matt laughed. "If you need an alibi, let me know."

"I just might take you up on that."

Matt waited for a few moments, but when it became clear Ashley wasn't going to calm down any time soon, he headed for the locker room. He wondered if he'd misread the signs. Maybe Caitlyn was just being polite. When he got to the door, he looked back toward the pool. Caitlyn was talking to Ashley, who nodded solemnly and then, theatrically summoning up her courage, put her head completely underwater. She held it there for half a second before coming up for air, a look of pride on her face. Caitlyn gave her a high five and then turned her attention to one of her other charges.

"Look at me. Look at me!" Ashley shrieked again.

Matt caught Caitlyn's eye as she turned back toward the little girl. He spread his fingers out in a semicircular shape and lowered his hand, as if he were pushing Ashley's head underwater. Caitlyn gave him two thumbs up, followed by a warm smile and a goodbye wave.

No, he said to himself. He wasn't misreading the signs. But he'd have to wait until next Tuesday to find out for sure.

"You did what?" Angela exclaimed, incredulous, when Matt and Sonya told her and Jesse how they got their hands on Harold Holt's file. "Do you realize that's breaking and entering?"

"You're kidding," Sonya said, pretending to be shocked.

"Detective Charney refused to let you see the files," Angela pointed out. "You had no right to be in the storage room."

"Isn't that trespassing?" Sonya asked.

"Not if you intended to commit a crime," Jesse said. "Like stealing something that doesn't belong to you." He sounded disapproving, but Matt could tell his heart wasn't in it. His heart was with Ray, 100 percent. "What's done is done," he said, confirming Matt's suspicion. "We're going to have to prove that Holt drank the Rolling Rock found at the Richardsons'. Was the bottle tested for fingerprints?"

"The police took it into evidence, but they never tested it," Sonya said.

"They wouldn't have bothered once Ray pled guilty," Angela said.

"How long will it take to do the test?" Matt asked.

"That depends on the district attorney," Jesse said. "It's his call. If he agrees to do it, it won't take more than a few days. But my guess is that we're going to have to go to court. Unless Holt confesses."

"Why would he confess?" Sonya asked.

"Same reason Ray did. To avoid the death penalty. Lonnie Shelton will make sure the DA takes the deal," Jesse explained, referring to the current state attorney general who had prosecuted the case against Ray when he was the district attorney in Snowden. "The last thing he's going to want is a long trial that will remind everybody he sent an innocent man to prison. I'll call our lawyer, Sean O'Brien, and have him get in touch with Holt's attorney."

He went into his cubicle, emerging a few minutes later. "Sean is going to speak to Holt's lawyer at five o'clock, when he gets out of court."

Matt looked at his watch. Ten thirty. It was going to be a long day.

"But even if Holt doesn't confess, Ray will still get out of jail, won't he?" Sonya asked.

"Yes, assuming Holt's fingerprints are on the beer bottle," Jesse said. But there was something in the way he said it that made Matt think he wasn't too worried about the test results. "We better not tell our investigators about this," he joked to Angela. "They work on cases for years without anything to show for it, and these two kids solve one in less than two months."

"Beginner's luck," Angela said.

True enough, Matt thought. Harold Holt was an ideal candidate for *America's Dumbest Criminal*. Only an idiot would bring a beer to a break-in and then hang around afterward to drink it.

Matt spent the rest of the day on the phone, talking football with the town's merchants and watching the minute hand on the clock slowly inch its way toward five o'clock.

Five fifteen came and went with no word from Sean. At five thirty Jesse and Angela sat down with Matt and Sonya and went through the agenda for the fundraiser. They were still at it when Jesse's phone finally rang.

"Hey, Sean." Three heads swiveled toward the phone. "How did it go with Holt's lawyer?" Jesse's face fell as he listened.

Crap, Matt thought. Holt wasn't going to confess. It was depressing to think it could be months before Ray was released from prison.

"Are you sure?" Jesse asked. "Yeah. I'll tell them," he said softly and ended the call. "Holt couldn't have done it."

"What?" Matt and Sonya shouted in unison.

"He was in the hospital when Gwen and Walter were killed. He got into a fight that morning. Somebody cracked his head wide open with a crowbar. He went to emergency at ten in the morning and didn't get out until noon the next day."

THIRTY-ONE

"I am not looking forward to this," Sonya said as she and Matt walked into Jolene's apartment building. Jesse had offered to be the bearer of the bad news, but Matt and Sonya felt it was their responsibility. They were the ones who had a relationship with Jolene, and they were the ones who had made the mistake of prematurely telling her about Harold Holt.

"I still can't believe Holt didn't do it," Sonya said.

"Me neither. But unless Harold Holt managed to sneak out of the hospital with his brains spilling out of his skull, he had nothing to do with the murders."

"I wonder…" Sonya started to say.

"What?"

"What if the real killer left the bottle of Rolling Rock in the kitchen to make the police think Walter and Gwen were killed by the same person who committed the break-ins? Jolene said Walter hardly ever drank beer."

"Hardly ever isn't never. And anyway, nobody knew about the Rolling Rock," Matt pointed out. "The police kept it secret, remember?"

"They didn't tell the public. But they knew about it."

"Are you seriously suggesting a policeman did this? Went to all that trouble to steal a few things that were hardly worth anything?"

"It was just a thought," Sonya said as she buzzed Jolene's apartment.

Jolene greeted them with a smile and a warm hug. "I want to show you something." She led them into the spare bedroom. The floor was covered with drop sheets. A man in white painter's coveralls was hammering the lid back onto a paint can. The ceiling and all four walls had a fresh coat of white paint.

"I'm all done for today, Mrs. Richardson," the painter said, heading for the door. "I'll come back tomorrow to put on a second coat."

"This is Ray's room," Jolene told Matt and Sonya. "I know white is boring, but I thought it was the safest choice. We can put prints on the wall to give the room some color, but I'll let Ray choose them. After all, he's the one who's going to have to live with them."

Matt and Sonya looked at each other. This was going to be harder than they'd thought.

"Is something wrong?" Jolene asked.

"Let's go into the living room," Sonya suggested.

"What is it?" Jolene asked anxiously after they were seated.

There was no gentle way to break the news. "Harold Holt didn't do it," Sonya said. "He was in the hospital when Walter and Gwen were killed."

Jolene stared at them blankly, as if she hadn't understood. "That can't be. That can't be."

Matt and Sonya stared at each other helplessly.

"I don't feel so good," Jolene said. She slumped in her chair, sweating profusely and gasping for air.

Sonya rushed to her side. "Call 9-1-1," she told Matt. "I think she's having a heart attack."

"That's not necessary," Jolene said weakly. "I don't have any pain in my chest."

Matt hesitated. "Do it!" Sonya ordered. She helped Jolene lie down on the couch and loosened her sweater while Matt described Jolene's symptoms to a dispatcher.

"The ambulance is on the way," he told Sonya after hanging up. "He says to give her an aspirin."

"In the medicine cabinet," Jolene murmured.

Matt rushed off, returning a moment later with an aspirin and a glass of water.

Sonya supported Jolene's head so she could swallow the pill. "You're going to be okay," she said calmly. She held Jolene's hand and talked to her reassuringly until the paramedics arrived ten minutes later.

Sonya accompanied Jolene to the hospital in the ambulance while Matt followed in Sonya's car.

"How did you know it was a heart attack?" he asked Sonya in the hospital waiting room. "She wasn't having any chest pain."

"Women often don't," Sonya said. "I took a first-aid course last summer. This is the first time I've had to use it."

"You were so cool. I was freaking out."

"Believe me, so was I."

An hour later Jolene's doctor, a youngish woman wearing a white lab coat, came toward them. Matt and Sonya got to their feet.

"Your grandmother had a mild heart attack," the doctor told Sonya, who had had the presence of mind to identify herself as Jolene's granddaughter, knowing the hospital would only release information to family members. "We're going to keep her under observation for a few days, but she's going to be fine."

Matt and Sonya hugged each other in relief.

"It's a good thing you called 9-1-1 right away," the doctor continued. "If you hadn't, she could have had a more serious attack later on. You probably saved her life. You can see her now. Your boyfriend can go with you."

"He's not—thanks," Sonya said.

Jolene was sleeping, her tiny frame dwarfed by the hospital bed. She was hooked up to an IV drip. A machine monitored her vital signs.

Matt looked at her sadly. It's our fault, he thought. They had given Jolene hope, and now it had been taken away. She would have been better off with no hope at all.

THIRTY-TWO

"Any word from Ralph?" Matt asked Sonya when he arrived at the office Monday morning.

She shook her head.

In the week since Jolene's heart attack, Ralph Chadwick had eliminated two of the three names on his list, leaving only one potential witness: Adrian Rice, who had lived directly across the alley from the Richardson house at the time of the murders.

Time for the Hail Mary, Matt thought as he sat down at his desk. It was a term they used in football—when your team was at midfield, needing a touchdown to win, with only enough time for one more play. They called it the Hail Mary after the Catholic prayer because your only chance was to throw the ball as far as you could and pray that someone on your team would catch it. You had a better chance of winning the lottery.

★ ★ ★

Matt and Sonya spent the day working on the fundraiser, then went to pick up Jolene, who had been staying at Lenore Patterson's house since she had gotten out of the hospital. Ray's grandmother hadn't suffered serious damage from her heart attack, but the doctors said she shouldn't be living alone. She had decided to move into a retirement home, and Matt and Sonya had volunteered to help pack up her apartment.

Jolene and Lenore were on the porch, talking to a middle-aged man with a neatly trimmed goatee specked with gray. Jolene didn't look as frail as she had at the hospital, but she didn't look a whole lot better either.

Lenore introduced her son, Leon, who was visiting from Brazil. "Matt and Sonya were the ones who emailed you about Ray's case."

"Sorry I wasn't able to be more help," Leon said.

"You're sure it was Ray you saw in the alley?" Matt asked.

"I'm sure. I was at home watching a movie. It's funny the details that stick in your mind. I can still remember what I was watching. *The Dirty Dozen*."

Matt nodded. He knew the movie, a war movie starring Jimmy Brown, one of the greatest running backs in NFL history. He'd seen it with his dad.

"After it was over I went upstairs to pack for a business trip. I looked out the window and saw Ray come through the back gate, wearing his Lakers hoodie." Leon smiled. "I think he wore it just to tick people off. Everyone around here is a

Celtics fan. Then he headed down the alley to Delaney, cool as a cucumber."

Cool as a cucumber. Like Oklahoma's quarterback, Jamelle Holieway. Matt reminded himself to choose some clips of Jamelle running the wishbone offense when he got home. Coach Bennett wanted to show them to the team before the first practice on Wednesday.

"Why didn't you tell the police you saw Ray?" Sonya asked.

"By the time I was back in town, he'd already pled guilty. There was no point driving another nail into the boy's coffin."

"Thank you so much for doing this," Jolene said when they got to her apartment. She had a defeated air about her, as if the disappointment over Harold Holt had finally squelched her spirit. "There's not much left to do. Lenore and Leon helped me get rid of a lot of stuff yesterday."

"Where should we start?" Sonya asked.

"I can only bring a few pieces of furniture into the retirement home. Everything else is going to the Salvation Army. Except that." She pointed to the cabinet with Walter's model-car collection. "I sold the cars to a collector in Harrisburg. Ralph Ellison. He was a friend of Walter's, so I know he's giving me a fair price."

There was no more mention of saving the collection for Ray, Matt noticed.

Jolene lowered herself onto the couch. She took a three-ring binder off the coffee table and handed it to Matt. "There's a list of the cars in here," she said. "I sent a copy to Ralph. That's how he was able to come up with a price. We should check to make sure it's accurate."

The binder had a master list and an information sheet for each car. Each sheet contained four color photographs of the car from different angles, along with typed notes under the heading *Aftermarket*.

"What does *Aftermarket* mean?" Matt asked.

"Those are the extras Walter put on the cars. He would never build them the way they came in the kit. He always customized them to make them more realistic."

Matt flipped through the binder. Walter *had* done something extra to every car. New headlights, disc brakes, seat belts...the list went on and on.

There looked to be close to fifty cars in the cabinet. They were all older models, most of which Matt and Sonya didn't recognize, but Walter had affixed a license plate with the year and the make on each.

After Jolene ticked a car off the master list, Matt and Sonya carefully wrapped the model in bubble wrap and packed it into a cardboard box. Four cars to a box.

"That's the last one," Sonya said when they were all done.

"Are you sure?" Jolene asked. "There should be one more. A 1959 Cadillac." She showed Matt and Sonya a picture of a bright-red convertible with huge tail fins like a rocket ship's.

"I didn't see it," Matt said. Sonya shook her head as well.

"I bet it was the movers," Jolene said. "A lot of stuff disappeared when I sold the house on Huntington Terrace. I'll have to let Mr. Ellison know, so he can adjust the price."

"Where should we put the cars?" Sonya asked.

"Put them in Ray's—in the spare room."

The spare room still smelled of fresh paint. Sonya sighed heavily. Matt put his hand on her shoulder, but he didn't say anything. There were no words that could make them feel better.

Matt boxed the photographs in the living room while Jolene and Sonya packed up the bedroom. He gazed at the picture of Jolene and Ray in front of the beach backdrop at the prison. It's the closest Ray will ever get to a beach, he thought.

When everything was done, the three of them walked to the front door. Jolene stopped at the doorway and took a last look around. "I lived here for fifty-six years," she said.

Then she closed the door behind her.

They had just dropped Jolene off at Lenore's house when Ralph Chadwick called. Matt was suddenly certain he was calling to say he'd found Adrian Rice and that Adrian had seen the real killer.

He was right on the first count but wrong on the second. Chadwick *had* managed to find Adrian. He was living in an off-the-grid commune in Washington State. But he hadn't seen a thing.

They had tried the Hail Mary. But their prayer had gone unanswered.

THIRTY-THREE

Matt had just finished his swim the next morning when the din of young voices echoed off the tiles, signaling the arrival of the Snowden Adventure Camp delegation. Caitlyn spotted him right away and greeted him with a wave and a smile. He noticed that her whiny camper, Ashley, was missing.

He waited until the kids were in the water and then swayed toward Caitlyn, dismissing the inner voice telling him not to make a fool of himself.

"I see you got away with it," he said.

"What do you mean?"

"No Ashley."

"If anybody asks, we went to a movie last night."

"I still can't believe you wouldn't share your popcorn with me."

Caitlyn laughed. "Ashley's sick today."

"Do you want to get together this weekend?" Matt blurted out.

"I'd love to."

"Really?" The word was out of his mouth before he could stop it. *Smooth move, dude.*

"You're cute. Yes, really."

Matt floated to the locker room. He turned around at the door. Caitlyn was talking to the lifeguard, but she was looking at him. She returned his wave with a beaming smile. Desire surged through his body like an electric current. He couldn't remember the last time he'd felt like this.

★ ★ ★

"So?" Sonya asked when Matt was at his desk.

"So what?"

"Was Caitlyn there?"

"She was."

"And?"

"And we're going out this weekend." He shrugged as if it was no big deal.

Sonya nodded knowingly. *Who do you think you're fooling?*

The front door opened, and a courier entered with a package. "It's the football jersey for the silent auction," Angela said, opening the box. "The school sent it over." She held it up. It was covered with signatures.

"If only I had an extra thousand dollars so I could bid on it," Sonya said dryly. Matt and Angela both laughed.

"You need to sign it too," Angela told Matt.

"Got to keep my fans happy," he said to Sonya as he got to his feet.

"You the man."

He scribbled his signature on the jersey. A heaviness settled over him as he looked at his name, surrounded by those of his former teammates. It was as if it belonged to someone else.

"Try it on," Angela said.

"That's okay," Matt said.

A moment later Jesse burst through the door. This time he didn't open and close it again. He was too excited.

"We just heard from the lab. They've identified the DNA on the bandanna found outside Bill Matheson's house. It belongs to a man named Alan Markwood."

"Fantastic," Angela said.

"It gets better. Markwood's a career criminal with a history of violence."

"Does this mean Bill's getting out?" Matt asked.

"It's just a matter of time. The DA will make things difficult, but there's no way he's going to be able to convince a judge that Bill is guilty. My guess is he'll be out by the end of the year."

Matt felt a mix of emotions. He was happy that Bill's nightmare was finally coming to an end, but the joy was tinged with despair. When Bill Matheson walked out of Pembroke Valley State Prison, Ray Richardson would still be locked up inside. And he'd be staying there for the rest of his life.

★ ★ ★

Matt didn't have any problem finding clips from the Oklahoma game tape to show the team. On play after play, Jamelle Holieway ran the wishbone to perfection. He really was cool as a cucumber.

That's when it hit him. Leon Patterson had said that Ray walked down the alley *cool as a cucumber*. But Ray said he'd run out of the house and down the alley in a complete panic.

Matt reached for his phone.

Leon confirmed what Matt suspected. He hadn't actually seen Ray's face. All he'd seen was someone wearing a Lakers hoodie.

Matt didn't know if he'd be able to find television listings from twenty-one years ago, but Google came through. The movie Leon had been watching, *The Dirty Dozen*, ended at four thirty. The basketball game Ray had watched at the Linsmore ended at five fifteen.

Leon didn't see Ray Richardson in the alley. He saw the real killer.

Matt reached for his phone again. It rang five times before Sonya answered.

"What's up?"

"Ray's innocent. And we can prove it."

THIRTY-FOUR

"How do you know Ray stayed at the bar until the basketball game ended?" Angela asked the next day when Matt and Sonya announced they'd cracked the case wide open.

"Because he won a bet on the game with the bartender," Matt said.

"Ray was at the Linsmore when Leon saw the killer leaving the Richardson house," Sonya said. "That proves he's innocent." She and Matt exchanged high fives.

"Let's not get ahead of ourselves," Jesse said, uttering familiar words of caution that put the brakes on the celebration. "We can't take Ray's word that he was at the bar when the game ended. We have to prove it." Then he pretty much ended the whole damn party. "And after all these years, that's not going to be easy to do."

★ ★ ★

Matt was on the bus, headed to the Linsmore to meet Sonya, when his dad called.

"How did practice go?"

"Coach Bennett liked the clips I chose, but being out on the field was tough," Matt said. "Tougher than I thought."

A lot tougher. Watching his former teammates run up and down the field had been a painful reminder of who he'd been. And his awkwardness each time he took a few steps to demonstrate the wishbone was an agonizing illustration of who he'd become.

"I wish I had some magic words to help you," his dad said. "But trust me. It will get easier."

"That's the theory," Matt said as the bus pulled up in front of the Linsmore, a squat red-brick building with grimy windows. "I gotta go. I'll see you at dinner."

Sonya was waiting outside. She stepped out of the way as a man in a plaid shirt stumbled out of the bar and burped loudly. "Nice place," she joked as Matt approached. "I'll have to come here with Morgan."

The Linsmore was as dingy inside as it was outside. The walls were painted dark brown, and the floor was covered with sawdust. It looked like it hadn't changed in the twenty-one years since Ray had been there, and probably not in the twenty-one years before that. Two men slumped on stools at a long bar manned by a bartender with a shaved head and a tattooed neck. Others sat at the scarred wooden tables, staring into their beers.

As if on cue, all eyes turned to Sonya. "I gotta stop drinking," one man called out. "I'm starting to hallucinate." The others laughed.

"Over here, honey," a burly man in a Celtics baseball cap shouted from a nearby table. "Got a seat right here for you." He patted his lap. Some of the other men hooted.

Two awkward steps brought Matt to the table. He glared down at the man. "What did you say?"

The room went silent. The man met Matt's eyes for a moment, then lowered his head. "Didn't mean anything by it," he muttered.

Matt gave him a final glare. His heart was beating a mile a minute.

"My hero," Sonya whispered as they walked over to the bar.

The bartender handed a glass of beer to one of his customers. He looked at Matt and Sonya, stone faced. "You got ID?"

The Linsmore is more law-abiding than it was in Ray's day, Matt thought.

"We don't want a drink," he said. "Does Skinny still work here?"

"Say what?"

"We're looking for a man named Skinny. He worked here about twenty years ago."

The bartender shook his head. "Never heard of him. You kids gotta go. I could lose my license if the cops find you in here."

"Can we talk to the owner?" Sonya asked.

"You're looking at him."

"Do you know anybody who was around back then?" Matt asked.

The bartender shook his head again. He pointed at the door.

"There must be somebody," Sonya pleaded. "It's important. A man's life is at stake."

The bartender laughed.

"It's not a joke," she snapped.

The bartender's smile disappeared. "Take it easy, darlin'."

"I'm not your darling, and I won't take it easy."

"We're not going anywhere until we get an answer," Matt said.

The bartender smirked and raised his hands in mock surrender. "Anybody remember a cat who used to work here, name of Skinny?" Everybody looked up momentarily before turning back to their beer. "Happy? Now get the hell out of here."

Sonya gave him a dirty look, and then she and Matt pivoted and headed to the door.

"What do you want with Skinny?" an old man asked as they passed his table. His ears stuck out sideways from his head.

"You want to talk to these kids, Jughead, you take it outside," the bartender called out angrily.

"No problem, Boss." Jughead got to his feet. He wasn't much taller standing up than he had been sitting down. "Dickweed," he whispered. "Skinny was a prince compared to that clown."

"Do you know where Skinny is?" Matt asked when they got outside.

"Last I heard he moved down south. Florida, I think."

"When was that?" Matt asked.

"Ten, fifteen years ago."

"Do you know his real name?"

"Nah. Everybody just called him Skinny. His brother's in the nursing home over on Barton."

"What's his name?" Matt asked.

"Shorty."

THIRTY-FIVE

The nursing home on Barton was called Ashland Gardens. A thin strip of pavement flanked by a few empty benches led to the front door. The closest thing to a garden was an urn near the entrance, sprinkled with a handful of wilted flowers.

The interior was equally depressing. A few patients were parked on faded furniture in the lobby, staring blankly at a TV blaring in the corner. Others watched from their wheelchairs. A man in a white uniform mopped the cracked linoleum floor.

"I've never been in one of these places before," Matt said.

"My grandma was in a nursing home for a year before she died," Sonya said.

"Was she the one Jolene reminds you of?"

Sonya nodded. "Good memory. She called it *God's waiting room*."

"Can I help you?" the receptionist asked.

"We're here to visit one of the patients," Sonya answered.

"We call them residents. What's the name?"

"Shorty. That's all we know."

"That would be Jim Thomas. Room 412."

"How's he doing?" Matt asked.

"Like everybody else. He has his good days and his bad days."

Matt and Sonya got off the elevator on the fourth floor. An old man slept in a ratty chair by the nursing station, his mouth open and a fleck of spittle on the corner of his lips. An old woman shuffled by in her pajamas, muttering to herself.

God's waiting room, Matt said to himself. It was hard to believe that all these ancient people were once his age. And even harder to believe that one day he would be theirs.

The television in room 412 was on, but the room was empty. A moment later an elderly man came out of the washroom across the hall. He stooped to get through the doorway. That'll be Shorty, Matt thought.

"Mr. Thomas?" Sonya asked.

The man broke into a big smile when he saw them. "My, my," he said to Sonya. "Look at you. All grown up. Last time I saw you, you were yay high." His hand trembled at his waist.

It took a couple of minutes before they gave up trying to explain to Shorty that Sonya wasn't his granddaughter Elaine.

"Is this your boyfriend?" he asked.

"We're just friends," Sonya said.

"Guess he's having one of his bad days," Matt whispered.

"We're looking for your brother, Skinny," Sonya said.

"He's down in Pensacola." Shorty pointed to a picture on his bedside table. "That's the two of us on the beach near his home." Matt suppressed a smile. Skinny had to weigh at least three hundred pounds.

"When's the last time you spoke to him?"

"A couple of days ago. We talk all the time."

"Do you have his phone number?" Matt asked.

"Yup." Shorty aimlessly rummaged through the desk drawer.

"Maybe it's in here," Matt said, picking up a dog-eared address book.

"That's it."

Skinny's number was scrawled beside his nickname. Matt entered it into his cell phone.

"You come see me again, Elaine," Shorty said. "And bring your boyfriend with you."

"That was easy," Sonya said as they walked down the hallway.

"Let's just hope Skinny remembers betting on the game with Ray. It was a long time ago," Matt said.

He waited until they were outside before making the call. The phone rang and rang and rang. He was about to give up when a woman answered the phone.

"Hello."

"May I speak to Tyrell Thomas, please?"

"Who's calling?" the woman asked angrily. Matt explained who he was. "Damn. Didn't Shorty tell you? Tyrell's dead."

"Dead?" Matt echoed.

"He passed two months ago. I guess I don't have to ask how Shorty's doing. What's this about?"

Two questions raced through Matt's head. Did Skinny tell his wife about losing the bet to Ray? And if he did, would it be admissible in a court of law?

He didn't get to question number two. Skinny's widow had never heard of Ray Richardson.

THIRTY-SIX

"How was your date with Caitlyn?" Sonya asked on Sunday morning. They were driving to the prison to see Ray, hoping he could come up with the name of somebody who could confirm he'd been at the Linsmore when the basketball game ended.

"Okay, I guess," Matt said.

"You going to see her again?"

"I don't think so. I don't see it going anywhere."

"Why not?"

"My limp freaks her out."

"She said that?"

"It's just a sense I got."

"If it bothered her, she wouldn't have gone out with you in the first place."

"I guess."

"Do you like her?"

"I do. She's funny and she's smart."

"And you said she was attractive."

"She is."

"Funny, smart, attractive. I can see why you don't want to go out with her again."

Matt's nerves were on edge as he and Sonya waited for Ray at a table in the visitors' room. There was a lot at stake. Unless somebody could corroborate Ray's alibi, he wouldn't be getting out of jail. And after all this time, it was a lot to hope for.

A banner that said *Bon Voyage Bill* was strung along the far wall, reminding Matt that Bill Matheson was getting out of jail the next day.

The news that Bill was innocent had hit his daughter, Heather, like a ton of bricks. At first, she'd told Jesse she didn't want to talk to her father. She felt too guilty, knowing she'd believed for all these years that he had killed her mother. But Jesse was able to persuade her that her father didn't blame her, and that night Bill spoke to his daughter for the first time in thirty-seven years.

Ray hurried over as soon as he saw Matt and Sonya. "Did something happen to Jolene?" he asked anxiously.

"She's fine," Sonya said, handing him a can of Coke.

"I'm real worried about her. I know the doctor said she'd be okay, but having a heart attack at her age, even a mild one, is scary."

"We should never have told her about Harold Holt," Matt said.

"Don't go blaming yourself."

Ray didn't show a flicker of emotion when he learned that Leon Patterson had seen the real killer, and he didn't show any when they told him Skinny was dead.

"Can you remember anyone else who was at the Linsmore that day?" Sonya asked.

Ray closed his eyes, stepping back in time. He shook his head. "I know there were other people there, but I can't come up with a face, let alone a name. All I remember is sitting at the bar, making fun of the Celtics after Skinny paid off on the bet. Knowing me, I probably made a real ass of myself." Judging from the look on his face, he could have been talking about the weather, as if it was no big deal that his only chance of getting out of jail had just gone up in smoke.

Matt felt the air go out of him. He'd expected as much, but it didn't make his disappointment any less acute.

"Does Jolene know about this?" Ray asked, draining the rest of his Coke. Matt shook his head. "Don't tell her. She's been through too much already."

"Would you like another drink?" Sonya asked.

"I won't say no," Ray answered. "I had a girlfriend who looked like her," he told Matt as Sonya headed to the vending machine. "Charlene Stewart. Sweet girl. She dumped me when I started doing drugs. Can't say I blame her. I wrote her once after I got here, but she never wrote back. Charlene Stewart," he repeated dreamily. "I haven't thought about her in a long time. You can't think about that stuff in here. It'll drive you crazy."

Matt thought about asking Ray if he would ever change his mind about seeking parole, but he knew the answer. *They can have my body, but they can't have my soul.* Matt didn't think he would ever understand. Ray had been his age when he went to prison. He had lived more than half his life behind bars. It blew Matt's mind that he would rather spend the rest of his life here than utter a few words that would give him back his life. And it broke his heart to think of Jolene making that long, lonely trek to the prison every two weeks for the rest of her life.

"Here you go," Sonya said, handing the can to Ray.

He cracked it open and took a swig. "I know sugar's the new tobacco, but damn, that tastes good." He gestured toward the banner. "We're having a party for Bill tonight. I'm happy for him, but I'm really going to miss him. He's been like a father to me." He turned back to Matt and Sonya. "When did Skinny die?"

"Two months ago."

"Two months," Ray said flatly. "Two months," he repeated, this time in anger. The realization that he had come so close to obtaining his freedom seemed to finally pierce his armor. He slammed his hand on the table. A guard looked over at him. Ray gave him a thumbs-up to show that everything was under control. Then he buried his face in his hands. When he removed them, the mask was back on. "You guys should get going. You got a long drive ahead of you."

"I wish we had better news," Matt said.

"Thank you for trying," Ray said as they all stood up. "It means a lot to know that people out there believe in me— that I'm not all alone." He stared solemnly at Sonya and shook her hand and then did the same with Matt. On his way out of the room, he stopped under the *Bon Voyage Bill* banner, turned toward them, gave a little wave and then disappeared through the door.

It was the saddest sight Matt had ever seen.

THIRTY-SEVEN

"There you go," Matt's dad said after adjusting the knot on Matt's tie. "You'll be the best-looking man at the fundraiser."

Matt checked himself out in the mirror. Not bad. His hard work at the pool had paid off. His blue suit with the herringbone pattern fit perfectly.

"You've been through a lot since you last wore it," his dad said.

Matt nodded. The last time was at the press conference when he and Anthony announced they were going to USC.

His dad was looking for his car keys when Matt noticed that his MVP trophy from the state championship was back on the top shelf of the cabinet, the football player standing on its pedestal.

"I didn't think you really wanted to throw it away," his dad said, catching his eye. "But we don't have to display it if you don't want to."

Matt took a closer look at the bronze figure. There was a line across the knees where his father had glued it back together. "No. I'm glad you kept it."

"I'm happy you didn't end up moving to Florida. I would have really missed you."

"I would have missed you too."

"No regrets?"

Matt shook his head. He remembered how he'd thought that things would be easier in Florida, where nobody knew who he was or what had happened to him. But it would have been harder. He couldn't have gotten through the past few months without the support of the people who cared about him. And, except for his mother, all those people were here in Snowden.

"Now give me a big smile," his father said, aiming his cell phone at Matt. He snapped the photo, then studied it. "I'm going to frame this and send it to your mom."

Matt got to the hotel an hour before the pre-dinner reception was due to start. The donated items were arrayed on long tables. The signed Falcons jersey was draped on a mannequin he had obtained from Teller's department store.

Sonya was going from table to table, putting name cards in place. She wore a plain white dress. Matt had never seen her look so beautiful, and that was saying something.

"You look sharp," Sonya said.

"You too. Wow. Are you sure I can't persuade you to change teams?"

"Ha ha."

At five o'clock the guests began to arrive. Matt tensed, anticipating an avalanche of stares.

"It's going to be fine," Sonya said. "In debating club they taught us a trick for dealing with nerves when you're in front of a crowd."

"What's that?"

"Imagine everyone in the audience is naked."

"Now I'm really scared," Matt said, gesturing at the parade of beefy adults making a beeline to the bar. Sonya laughed.

They were standing near the door when the mayor and her husband arrived.

"Jesse brought me up to date on Ray's case," Jamie said. "It's heartbreaking, just heartbreaking. I can't imagine what he's going through. Do you think he'll ever apply for parole?"

"Not a chance," Matt said.

"I'd like to visit him, just to let him know he's not alone, but it's been so many years since I've seen him. I don't know how he'd feel about it."

"I'm sure it would mean a lot to him," Sonya said.

"You can come with us the next time we take Jolene," Matt offered.

"It would be less awkward that way," Dan Burke pointed out.

"Jolene wouldn't mind?" Jamie asked.

"She'd be delighted," Sonya said.

Jamie wasn't the only one to convey her regrets about Ray's plight. Sean O'Brien, the Justice Project's lawyer, and Doug Cunningham, Ray's trial lawyer, both commiserated with Matt and Sonya. They knew what it felt like to put your heart and soul into a noble cause only to come up short. "The hardest lesson I've had to learn," Sean said, "is to accept that life isn't always fair without giving in to despair—without giving up the fight."

Amen, Matt thought.

"How do you like coaching?" Doug Cunningham asked.

"It's not as much fun as playing," Matt admitted. He was still trying to adjust to his new role. It hadn't taken long to realize that the players didn't care about his limp—they knew he could help them improve, and that was all that mattered—but it was going to take a lot longer than two weeks before he stopped thinking about what might have been.

He had just gotten an orange juice for himself and a sparkling water for Sonya when the Chief arrived.

"I wonder what he'd say if he knew that we'd thought he killed Ray's parents," Sonya said.

"One look and he'd forgive you," Matt said, leering at Sonya in his best impression of a dirty old man. "He'd have *me* put in an insane asylum. I was so sure he did it. Everything fit, except for the fact that he was seven hundred miles away."

"Occam's razor," Sonya said.

"Say what?"

"Occam's razor. We learned about it in philosophy class. It's a rule that says the simplest solution to a problem is usually the right one. All those clues—*the shit is going to hit the fan*, the Rolling Rock beer, Harold Holt—they kept us from seeing the obvious explanation. A burglar broke into the Richardsons' house and killed Walter and Gwen when they came home. It's as simple as that."

A loud cheer erupted when Bill Matheson arrived with Jesse and Angela. Bill was immediately swarmed. He towered above everybody, looking ill at ease with all the attention.

Matt attracted a fair bit of attention himself. It was a week before the season opener, and everybody had an opinion about the team's prospects—and they all were exceedingly generous in sharing it. Matt was relieved when everyone was told to go to the dining room.

After they were all seated, Jesse introduced Bill and recounted the circumstances of his wrongful conviction. Everybody applauded when Jesse told them about Bill's refusal to apply for parole. And when Jesse quoted his explanation—*they can have my body, but they can't have my soul*—the audience rose in a standing ovation, although Matt suspected that the man at the next table, who muttered, "You've got to be kidding," wasn't the only one who questioned Bill's sanity.

At the end of the evening Jesse called Matt to the podium to announce the successful bidders in the silent auction. He tried to keep Sonya's tip in mind as he lurched across the floor, but it felt like he was the one who was naked.

The auction exceeded expectations. Just about every item went for more than its actual value. The Sleazebucket walked away with the signed Falcons jersey, but it cost him $1,900.

Matt presented the jersey to the Chief, who handed it to Jamie. "I always wanted a football player in the family," he joked as she put it on. He summoned the *Sentinel*'s photographer, who snapped a shot of the mayor and Matt standing next to each other. "Front page of tomorrow's paper," the Chief predicted.

"You can't buy that kind of publicity," Dan Burke said approvingly.

After dinner everybody mingled. The room was stuffy. Matt stepped onto the balcony to get some air.

Bill Matheson was standing by the railing, taking in the view. "This is going to take some getting used to," he said. "Normally by this time, I'd be in my cell for the night."

"Jesse said you're moving to Seattle."

"Yeah. Heather wants me to live with her and her kids. The last time I saw her, she was fifteen years old. I've never even seen a picture of my grandchildren." He looked at Matt. "You're wondering if I regret not taking parole."

Matt nodded.

"I never did, and I never will," Bill said forcefully. "My innocence is what kept me going all these years. If I'd given that up, I'd have gotten out of jail, but I wouldn't have been free. In the eyes of the world I would be a murderer. And I would never have gotten my family back. Well, I guess I better get back in there before they send out a search party."

Matt watched Bill shuffle back into the hall. He had paid an awful price for his decision, but at least he was at peace with it. Matt wondered if Ray would be able to say the same when he was Bill's age.

THIRTY-EIGHT

"I'm looking forward to seeing the house," Sonya said to Matt the next day, as they arrived at Lawson House for the cocktail party. "I read that Jamie and Dan spent half a million dollars on the renovations."

"What time do you think we'll be done?" Matt asked.

"I don't know. Why?" She looked at him and smiled. "You're seeing Caitlyn again."

"I am."

It had taken him a few days to summon up the nerve to call her. Her first words had put his fear of rejection to rest. *I was hoping you'd call,* she said.

"Look at that view," Sonya said when they were inside the house. Floor-to-ceiling windows showcased a large backyard with a spectacular garden, surrounded by an ivy-covered wall. In the distance a forest extended as far as the eye could see.

"Not too shabby," Matt agreed.

About twenty-five guests milled about in the living room. The Chief, wearing the Falcons sweatshirt he'd reclaimed from Jamie, was talking to a good-looking young woman. Old habits die hard, thought Matt.

A uniformed server held out a tray of appetizers. "Fiery grilled shrimp with honeydew gazpacho," he announced. Matt and Sonya helped themselves.

"How good is that?" Matt asked. Sonya nodded happily.

They corralled server after server. Foie gras with date purée and pomegranate. Prosciutto-wrapped grissini. Potato croquettes with saffron aioli. It was all as delicious as it sounded, even if Matt wasn't always quite sure what he was eating.

He was sampling a fig stuffed with goat cheese when Sonya pointed to a wedding picture on the wall.

"Dan looks old enough to be Jamie's father," she said. Jamie must have been in her twenties in the photo, but she looked like a high-school student. Burke, on the other hand, was already going bald. "I wonder what the Chief said when Dan finally told him he was going out with his daughter."

"I'm glad to see we have something in common?" Matt suggested.

Sonya laughed.

Matt was chasing down another server when he saw Jamie talking to Bill Matheson. Bill waved him over. He was holding a model car, a long, sleek convertible.

"I bet you've never seen one of these," Bill said. "A '64 Thunderbird. This is the car I wanted when I was your age."

Matt nodded, but he wasn't listening. His gaze was drawn to the dozens of model cars in a display cabinet behind Bill. It's just a coincidence, he told himself. *Thousands of people collect model cars. So what if Dan Burke is one of them? It doesn't mean anything.*

But that didn't stop Matt from sweeping his eyes along the shelves, looking for the red Cadillac with rocket-shaped tail fins that had gone missing from Walter Richardson's collection. It only took a few seconds to see it wasn't there. Give it up, dude, he told himself. But he took a second look just to be sure.

Bill put the Thunderbird back in the cabinet. "How long has your husband been building model cars?" he asked Jamie.

"He started when he was a boy. He built himself a workshop in the basement. I'd be embarrassed to tell you how much it cost."

Bill took another car out of the cabinet. It reminded Matt of the cars in old black-and-white movies.

Dan Burke strolled over to them.

"My dad drove a car like this," Bill told him.

"A '48 Packard. It's a classic. Are you a car enthusiast as well, Matt?"

"I'm just along for the ride," Matt said. Everybody laughed. It took him a moment to realize he'd made a pun.

"You should show Bill the rest of your collection," Jamie said to her husband.

Matt's ears perked up.

"I'd love to see it," Bill said.

"How long are you staying in town?" Burke asked.

"I'm here for another week."

"Great. Why don't you come by before you leave?"

"Would tomorrow be convenient?"

Burke shook his head. "I go to Leamington to visit my father every Sunday. It's a couple of hours away, so I'll be gone all day."

"You're a good son," Bill said approvingly. Matt wondered if he was thinking of all the Sundays he didn't get to spend with Heather.

"I'll call you Monday, and we'll set something up," Burke said. He turned to Jamie. "You should make your pitch now, before people start leaving."

Burke called for everybody's attention, then turned the floor over to Jamie.

"I want to thank you for coming," Jamie said. "You all heard Bill Matheson's story…"

Matt tuned out. Was it possible Burke had Walter's Cadillac? That he'd stolen it after killing Walter and Gwen? But that made no sense. Burke had no reason to kill Ray's parents. Matt was letting his imagination run away with him. Just like he had with the Chief. He'd been dead certain that the Chief had driven the car in the fatal hit-and-run and had killed Walter to stop the truth from coming out. Dead certain and dead wrong.

He checked his phone. It was six thirty. He texted Caitlyn.

Almost finished here. Meet you at 7:30?

Yay. c u then

Matt turned his attention back to Jamie, who invited Bill to say a few words.

Bill kept it short and sweet. "I wouldn't be here today if it wasn't for the Justice Project. But there are lots of people who still need their help. So please help." He paused for a moment, fighting back emotion. "That's all I have to say."

"There's only more item on the agenda," Jamie told the crowd. "Your donation."

"Pick your favorite number and then add a few zeros," her husband suggested. Everybody laughed dutifully. Burke put his arm around Jamie's shoulders.

He still looks old enough to be her father, Matt thought. *Oh my god.* His mind was reeling as if he'd been struck by lightning. *The Chief wasn't driving the car. Burke was. And the young girl in the passenger seat wasn't one of the Chief's girlfriends. It was Jamie.*

It all fit. When Walter read the article in the *Sentinel* and realized the Chief's car was involved in the hit-and-run, he would have assumed that Jamie was the passenger—she was the only person other than the Chief who had access to the car—and that the driver was one of her many boyfriends. It wouldn't have occurred to him that Burke was the driver, because he and Jamie had kept their relationship a secret. Walter didn't call Burke to see if the Chief needed him. He called to tell him that the Chief's daughter had been involved in a fatal hit-and-run.

Substitute Burke for the Chief, and the rest of the story unfolded the way he and Sonya had envisioned. Burke told Walter to come to Lawson House and then accompanied him back to the Richardson house, where he killed Walter. When Gwen came home, he killed her too. Then he staged the fake burglary, left behind the bottle of Rolling Rock to steer the police in the wrong direction, put on Ray's Lakers hoodie so nobody would see he was covered in blood, grabbed the red Cadillac and walked out of the house. *Cool as a cucumber.*

He hurried over to Sonya.

"Tell me I'm crazy," he said after he'd laid out his theory.

"If you're crazy, I'm crazy. We've got to be here when Burke shows Bill the rest of his collection. But how are we going to manage that?"

"I have no idea."

The guests handed in their donations and headed off. Within a few minutes everybody had departed except for the hosts and the Justice Project contingent.

"Thanks for doing this," Jesse said to Jamie and her husband. "I can't tell you how much we appreciate it. We're going to be able to help a lot of innocent men and women."

"I'll call you Monday and set up a time to show you the cars," Burke said to Bill.

"Why don't you show them to Bill now and save him the trip?" Jamie suggested.

"I don't want to hold up Jesse and Angela," Bill said.

Matt leaped on the opening. "Sonya and I can drive you back to your hotel."

"Done," Burke said with a smile.

"I'll leave you to it," Jamie said after Jesse and Angela left. "Good night."

Burke led the others to his study. "Jamie calls this my man cave," he joked. A black leather couch with two matching armchairs faced a gigantic TV screen. The television was flanked by built-in floor-to-ceiling shelves that housed the rest of Burke's massive collection.

"Is that a '71 Mustang?" Bill asked, pointing to a lime-green convertible.

"A '72," Burke answered. "I put a new engine in it." He took it off the shelf and opened the hood, exposing a shiny chrome engine.

"Beautiful."

Bill took his time looking at the collection, showing genuine appreciation for the work Burke had done, while Matt scanned the shelves slowly, from left to right, top to bottom. There were several red cars, but there was no Cadillac with rocket-shaped tail fins. He scanned the shelves again. Nothing.

Sonya stood by his side. "Occam's razor."

"Occam's razor."

THIRTY-NINE

"One, two, three. Break," Matt called out, clapping his hands, as he and his teammates ran out of the huddle. He lurched forward and took his place behind the center. He wondered why he was wearing a Los Angeles Lakers hoodie instead of his football jersey.

Anthony Blanchard stood on the left side of the field. "What are you waiting for?" he shouted. Matt looked at him helplessly. He couldn't remember what play they were supposed to run.

The referee blew his whistle. "Delay of game," he said.

Anthony ran toward him. He angrily jabbed Matt in the shoulder. "The needle's going right there, asshole." The referee blew his whistle again. And then again. And again...

Matt woke with a start. He turned off his alarm and stared at the ceiling, waiting for his heart to stop pounding. He felt as helpless as he had in his dream.

He and Sonya had been on a roller coaster all summer, trying to free Ray, but the ride was over. It ended five days ago in Dan Burke's man cave. But it was going to take a lot longer than five days to come to terms with the disappointment.

A text from Caitlyn put the brakes on his descent into despair.

Had a great time last night.

Me too, he texted back. **Have fun at Grandma's.** Caitlyn was spending the weekend with her grandmother in Pittsburgh.

Good luck tonight. A reference to the Falcons' season opener.

Thanks. See you Monday.

His date with Caitlyn had been full of surprises.

Surprise number one had come when they left Greg's with their ice cream cones after seeing a movie. There was the usual foot traffic on Park Street and, as usual, everybody glanced at Matt's limp before pretending it didn't exist.

"Does that bother you?" Caitlyn asked. It was the first time the subject of his leg had come up.

"I'm used to it," he answered. "Does it bother you?"

"I'll get used to it," she said and then slipped her arm through his.

Surprise number two had come while he was walking her home. He was wondering whether he should kiss her good night when she stopped in her tracks. "Let's kiss now and get that out of the way," she said. He could still remember the taste of black-cherry ice cream on her lips.

Surprise number three was the fact that he hadn't thought about Emma all night. Except for one moment, when he saw a girl who looked like Emma's friend Rona boarding a bus across the street from Greg's.

Sonya was putting some files in order when he arrived at the office. "I can't believe it's our last day," she said.

"Yeah."

They lapsed into silence. Matt was thinking about Ray, and he was pretty sure Sonya was too. But neither of them said anything, as if they had an unspoken agreement not to mention him. "When do you head to Boston?" he asked.

"Monday. You should come visit me. It'd be fun."

"For sure."

"What are you doing tonight?" Sonya asked.

"You clearly don't keep up with the news. It's our first game. I can comp you a ticket. One of the perks of the job."

"I'd love to, but I promised my dad I'd stay home to make sure nobody steals the lawn."

Matt was cleaning out his desk when he found, buried at the back of the drawer, the *Sentinel's Sunday Magazine* with the cover image of Jamie Jenkins on the front steps of the newly renovated Lawson House. He was about to throw it out when he remembered it contained Violet Bailey's article on the death penalty that Jesse had recommended. He put it in his backpack. He didn't need any more convincing about the need to eliminate the death penalty, but he'd decided to study criminology at Eastern State, and it might come in handy for his criminal law course.

Jesse and Angela treated them to lunch at Bellini's, one of the best restaurants in town. "We can't tell you how pleased we are with the job you did all summer and especially on the fundraiser," Jesse said after everyone had ordered.

"We brought in over seventy-five thousand dollars," Angela said.

"We'll be able to double our case load," Jesse added. He paused. He knew what Matt and Sonya were thinking. Ray's case wasn't one of them. "I wish we could help Ray, but there's nothing we can do."

"I know how disappointed you are," Angela said. "You did everything you could, if that's any consolation."

Matt and Sonya exchanged a look. It wasn't.

"This place won't be the same without you," Jesse said, moving on.

"Hear, hear," Angela said. "We've got a gift for each of you to thank you for all your hard work." She handed a small gift-wrapped package to Sonya and an envelope to Matt.

Sonya opened her present. A pair of dangly earrings and a matching bracelet. "These are beautiful. Thank you."

Matt's gift was a pair of tickets to the New England Patriots opening game. "This is perfect. My dad's birthday is coming up, and I had no idea what to get him. This is going to blow him away."

Matt and Sonya had nothing to do at the office, but they hung around with Jesse and Angela for a while longer, reluctant to leave the summer behind.

"Do you want to get a coffee?" Matt asked Sonya when they finally left.

"I can't. I told Jolene I'd drop by to see her."

"My dad said I could have the car next weekend. Tell her I'll take her to see Ray then."

"Don't forget to invite Jamie."

"I won't. I guess this is goodbye," Matt said.

"I'll be back at Thanksgiving."

"You know what I mean."

Sonya nodded. The two of them had given everything they had in an effort to prove Ray was innocent. They had been together every step of the way, sharing their joy when it appeared that they had succeeded, and their sorrow when they realized they had failed. But now the journey had ended, and they were moving on. Life was taking them in different directions.

"You take care, Matt," Sonya said.

"You too."

They hugged, and then Sonya got into her Honda and drove off. Matt watched until the car had disappeared from sight.

★ ★ ★

It's going to be a long season, Matt thought as he watched the locker-room celebration after the Falcons' victory in the season opener. It was gratifying to know he had made a contribution to the win, but standing on the sidelines wasn't the same as being out on the field in the middle of the action, with the cheerleaders shouting his name and fourteen thousand fans cheering his every move. Not even close.

He slipped out of the locker room and headed home. Traffic on Park Street was bumper to bumper. Horns honked. People yelled to each other through car windows. It was football season again, and Snowden had come back to life.

The bus came to a stop in front of Charlie's Diner. The framed copy of the *Sentinel*'s front page with its giant headline—*STATE CHAMPS! Barnes Leads Falcons to the Promised Land*—was still in the window.

Matt regarded it neutrally, as if the Matt Barnes in the newspaper was somebody else, somebody he once knew long ago. The bus started up again. A chapter in his life had ended. A new one was about to begin.

It was time to turn the page.

FORTY

Matt slept in late the next morning. He had a couple of hours to kill before going to The Goon's house. The guys were getting together to watch Anthony Blanchard's first game in a USC uniform. It was on national television.

If only.

Matt put a load of clothes in the washing machine, tidied up his desk so it would be ready for school, and then emptied his backpack. He took out the *Sentinel's Sunday Magazine* and began reading Violet Bailey's article on the death penalty.

It blew his mind from the opening paragraph. He'd had no idea that executions could be so gruesome, and Violet hadn't spared the grisly details: bodies that caught fire when the electric chair failed to function properly, executions that required numerous jolts of electricity before the condemned man finally expired amid the stench of singed flesh, improperly administered lethal injections that left men moaning in pain for more than an hour before they finally died. Matt knew that most of these men had been guilty, and that they had shown absolutely no compassion toward their victims, but that didn't justify the barbaric way they had been treated.

But the botched executions, a relative rarity, weren't the part of the article that shocked Matt the most. That came when he read that a black man convicted of murder was four times more likely to be sentenced to death than a white man who committed the same crime. The color of the victim made a difference as well. If the victim was white, there was a far greater chance that his or her killer would be sentenced to death than if the victim came from a racial minority. Some lives clearly mattered more than others.

He was digesting these troubling facts when Emma called. His heart leaped, as it always did when he saw her name on the screen.

"How did the tour go?" he asked. Emma had been on tour with the theater company for the past two weeks.

"Tiring but exciting. I hear you've been a busy boy."

"You spoke to Rona." It *had* been her across the street from Greg's.

"Rona said she was really cute. What's her name?" Emma sounded disturbingly undisturbed.

"Caitlyn. And she is. Really cute."

"Is it serious?"

"We've only been on three dates."

"That's not an answer."

"It's got potential."

"That's great. I'm really happy for you, Matt." Too happy, he thought. "It makes it a lot easier to tell you what I've got to tell you. I've been seeing someone too. His name's Max. He's one of the other actors."

"Is it serious?"

"It's got potential."

"That's great," Matt said, with an enthusiasm he didn't wholly feel. Even though he was excited about the way things were going with Caitlyn, it still bothered him to think of Emma with someone else. "I hope he knows how lucky he is."

"I hope so too, because I keep telling him."

Matt laughed.

"How's Ray's case going?" Emma asked.

"Not good." He brought Emma up to date.

"That's horrible. The poor man."

"It's a freaking nightmare. We know Ray's innocent, and we can't do a damn thing about it."

"It must be incredibly frustrating. But I'm glad to see you like this."

"Like what?"

"It's been a long time since you were this passionate about something. I know you're upset—"

"That's putting it mildly."

"—but feeling something is a lot better than not feeling anything at all."

★ ★ ★

Matt thought about Emma's comment after they said goodbye. He remembered how depressed he'd been before he started working on Ray's case, how hopeless life had seemed, how hard it had been just to get out of bed in the morning. But he didn't feel like that now. He recalled what Angela had said on his first day at the Justice Project, how fighting for Jesse had given her a purpose. Fighting for Ray had done the same for him. It had given him something to focus on other than himself.

He knew his struggles were far from over. He knew it would be a long time before he fully came to terms with what had happened to him, before he stopped seeing himself as a victim. But at least there was light at the end of the tunnel.

He picked up the magazine and idly turned the pages until he came to the photo spread showing the renovations to Lawson House. He flipped through the pictures. Room after room decked out in luxury. So that's what half a million bucks gets you, he thought.

The last picture showed Dan Burke in his state-of-the-art workshop. He stood in front of his workbench, holding the same lime-green Ford Mustang he'd shown them in his study. The hood was open, revealing the shiny chrome engine he had so proudly installed. Matt cringed when he remembered how ready he and Sonya had been to accuse him of murder. He was about to turn the page when a flash of color caught his eye.

A red Cadillac with rocket-shaped tail fins sat on a shelf behind Burke's left ear.

Matt reached for his phone and called The Goon to say he wouldn't be able to come over to watch Anthony's game. Then he called Sonya.

★ ★ ★

An hour later they were in Jolene's room in the retirement home, watching her study the photo of Dan Burke in his workshop. Showing it to her wasn't a decision they had taken lightly. They both remembered what had happened the last time they'd given Jolene hope. But there was no way of doing what they had to do without her.

"It could just be a coincidence," Sonya said. "It might not be Walter's car."

"You don't believe that for a minute, and neither do I," Jolene said.

"What changes did Walter make to the car?" Matt asked.

Jolene retrieved the three-ring binder and turned to the information sheet for the 1959 Cadillac. "He added red flocking and put on a new license plate," she said.

"What's flocking?" Matt asked.

"It's a powder you glue on the floor of the car that looks like carpeting." Then she cut to the chase. "How are you going to get into Burke's workshop?"

"We've got a plan," Matt said.

"Are you sure you're up to this?" Sonya asked after she and Matt had laid out their scheme.

Jolene replied with a voice as hard as steel. "Don't you worry about me."

FORTY-ONE

At eight thirty the next morning Sonya dropped Matt off at
the south entrance of Ross McNaughton Park. He walked
through the park to the north entrance and found a spot that
gave him an unobstructed view of Lawson House. There was
nothing to do now but wait.

At nine fifteen Dan Burke drove his white Mercedes out
of the garage and turned left, on his way to Leamington to
visit his father. Matt texted Sonya.

Good to go.

A few minutes later Sonya pulled into the semicircular
drive at Lawson House. She and Jolene got out of the car,
walked to the front door and rang the bell. Jamie opened the
door, purse in hand, ready to go see Ray. She shook hands
with Jolene, the two women chatted briefly, and then they all
went into the house.

So far, so good, Matt thought. Even though he hadn't
heard the conversation, he knew the gist of it. Jolene had told

Jamie she'd seen the photo spread of Lawson House in the *Sentinel,* and Jamie had offered to give her a tour.

Matt went back into waiting mode, trying not to think about the various ways the plan could unravel. Twenty minutes crept by before the three women finally emerged. Sonya ran her right hand through her hair as Jamie locked up. *We're on.*

Sonya and Jolene had done their jobs. The rest was up to Matt.

He left the park and circled around to the forest behind Lawson House. It would have been easy to get lost, but the markers on the orienteering map Sonya had prepared the day before were easy to find, and he had no problem retracing their route. Fifteen minutes later he spotted the moss-covered log that had fallen into a small stream. He turned left and clambered up the hillside.

The ladder was where he and Sonya had left it, hidden in the bushes by the wall at the rear of Lawson House. Matt leaned it against the wall, climbed up and peered into the backyard to make sure the coast was clear. He pulled the ladder up, placed it against the other side of the wall and then clambered down into the garden.

He entered the kitchen through the sliding glass doors that Sonya had unlocked while Jamie was giving Jolene the tour. He reminded himself that he had plenty of time— Jamie wouldn't get back from the prison for at least six hours, and Burke would be gone just as long—but that didn't make him feel any less jumpy. If he got caught, he could go to prison. But it was either take the risk or condemn Ray to a life behind bars. And that was a no-brainer.

He took some deep breaths to steady himself, then went down to the basement. He walked into Burke's wine cellar before he found the workshop.

The Cadillac was on a shelf, right where it had been in the picture in the *Sentinel* magazine. 1959 *Cadillac* was imprinted on the license plate, and the car floor was covered with red flocking. It was exactly what Matt had expected to see, but his body quivered with excitement nonetheless.

Using his cell phone, he snapped a few pictures of the car on the shelf, making sure they showed the red flocking and the license plate, so that Burke wouldn't be able to claim that it wasn't his. Then he removed a large clear plastic bag from his backpack. He put on a pair of latex gloves, took hold of the Cadillac with his fingertips and slipped it into the plastic bag, just like the detectives did on TV.

He felt giddy with excitement. They'd done it. They'd really done it.

He was about to go back upstairs when the front door slammed shut. He heard footsteps overhead. A phone rang. The footsteps stopped at the top of the stairs to the basement. Matt's heart was pounding so hard, he thought it was going to pop right out of his chest.

"I'm back at the house, Dad." Matt recognized Burke's voice. "I was on the road when you called to say you wanted the picture of you and Mom in Yosemite. Remember?... I know you miss her. I miss her too." Burke's gentle treatment of his father took Matt by surprise. It wasn't what you'd expect from a double murderer.

The footsteps resumed, moving away from the stairs. Matt exhaled. A short while later the front door slammed shut again. He waited a few more minutes to make sure Burke wasn't coming back and then headed upstairs.

"Stop right there," a voice commanded.

Matt turned. Burke had a gun in his hand, pointed right at Matt.

It was hard to say who was more surprised.

FORTY-TWO

"What are you doing here?" Burke asked.

"I was just..." Matt's voice trailed off. He couldn't think of anything to say.

"Get on your knees, and slide the backpack over here," Burke said, the gun aimed squarely at Matt's chest.

Matt did as he was told. *How did Burke know somebody was in the house? Did I forget to close the sliding glass doors?*

Burke unzipped the backpack and extracted the plastic bag containing Walter's Cadillac. "What the ...? How did you know about this?" He seemed genuinely perplexed. Matt didn't answer. "Stand up and turn around."

Matt obeyed. The sliding glass doors were closed. How did he know? Matt asked himself again.

"When I saw the ladder, I thought a thief had broken into the house," Burke said. "I guess I was right."

Matt looked through the floor-to-ceiling windows. He felt the air go out of him. There it was, leaning against the wall at the rear of the property. *The ladder. The freaking ladder.* It hadn't occurred to him to hide it. There had been no need, not with everybody out of the house.

Burke stuck the gun into Matt's back and propelled him into the kitchen. "On the floor. Face down."

Matt lay down. Out of the corner of his eye he watched Burke open a drawer and take out a roll of duct tape.

"Put your hands behind your back." Burke tore off a length of tape and wound it around Matt's wrists before rolling Matt over onto his back. "I thought it was odd when you showed so much interest in my model-car collection at the cocktail party. But it never crossed my mind that you knew about Walter's car. How did you figure it out?"

"Fuck you."

"You've been watching too many movies." Burke's phone rang. He covered Matt's mouth with a piece of tape. "Hi, Dad. What's up?...Mom can't come to the phone right now. She's working in the garden. She'll call you later." He put the phone back in his pocket and shook his head sadly. "Old age isn't for sissies. Get up." He helped Matt to his feet and steered him down the hallway and into a two-car garage.

Jamie's convertible occupied one of the spots. Burke ordered Matt to lie down on the floor and then wrapped duct tape around his ankles. He pushed a button on the wall, opening the garage door, and stepped out of Matt's line of sight. Matt squirmed, desperately trying to get to his feet, but it was impossible. Burke backed his Mercedes into the garage. For a panicked moment Matt thought he was going to get run over, but the car stopped a foot away. The garage door closed. Burke got out of his car and walked back into the house through the door to the kitchen. A couple of minutes later he returned with a duffel bag.

He bent down and took Matt's cell phone out of his pocket. "Sonya must be wondering what's happening," he said. He began tapping away. "We...were...wrong," he said as he texted. "The Cadillac isn't Walter's. Say hi to Ray."

Matt's phone buzzed almost immediately. Burke checked the text. "What's Occam's razor?" he asked. He tossed the phone into the duffel bag, popped open the trunk of the Mercedes and pulled Matt to his feet. "Sit," he said, gesturing at the edge of the trunk.

Matt shook his head. *No freaking way.*

"We can do this the easy way or the hard way," Burke said, brandishing the gun. "Do what I say, and you won't get hurt."

There was no point resisting. Burke lifted Matt's legs, turning him to the side, and helped him into the trunk. Then he closed the trunk, and day turned to night.

The engine started, and the car moved forward. It turned left out of the driveway. Burke still intended to visit his father in Leamington, Matt reasoned, but that was as far as logic would take him.

He wondered if Burke had meant it when he said he wasn't going to hurt him. He'd sounded sincere, but then again, didn't psychos always sound sincere? How could Burke let him go when he knew what Matt knew?

They had driven for what Matt guessed was half an hour—but it could have been half that or twice that—when the car turned onto a rough road and slowed to a crawl. Sheer terror engulfed Matt. He forced himself to breathe, trying to push away the panic. A short while later the car came to a stop. The trunk popped open. Matt blinked as his eyes adjusted to the light.

Burke was silhouetted against the sky. Before Matt could see where he was, Burke slipped a hood over his head. Darkness descended once more. Burke helped Matt out of the trunk and steadied him on his feet. He cut the tape that bound Matt's legs, led him a few steps forward and then stopped. A door creaked open. He steered Matt a few more steps, sat him down on a dirt floor with his back against a wall and retied Matt's ankles with the duct tape.

"This would never have happened if that stupid woman hadn't jumped in front of the car," Burke whined. "She came out of nowhere. What was I supposed to do? I'd had a couple of drinks. If I'd called the police, I would have gone to jail. And for what? It wouldn't have brought her back to life. Nobody would have ever found out if Walter hadn't seen the article and put two and two together.

"Here's what's going to happen. I'm going to do some work on Walter's car, so nobody will be able to prove it was his. When I'm done, I'm going to go visit my dad. Then I'll come back here, get the model car—the glue will be dry by then—and put it in my workshop. Then I'll come back for you and drop you off on the outskirts of town. At that point you'll have a choice to make. You can accuse me of murder without a shred of evidence, and have everybody in town think you're a deranged nutbar, or you can keep your mouth shut and get on with the rest of your life."

Matt heard something—the duffel bag?—being unzipped, followed by sounds he couldn't identify but which, he knew, meant Burke was putting his plan into motion. He didn't know the techniques Burke was using to accomplish his task, but the end result was no mystery: no trace of red flocking, and a new license plate.

Matt racked his brain, looking for a hole in Burke's plan— something he had overlooked, something that would prove Burke had killed Walter and Gwen. But he came up empty. It would be his word against Burke's, and without any proof to back him up, nobody would believe him. Burke would get away with his crime, and Ray would never get out of jail.

"I'll be back in a few hours," Burke said after a while. "That should give you plenty of time to decide how you want to play this."

A few seconds later the car door opened and closed, and the engine started. Car wheels crunched on gravel, then faded away until the only sounds Matt could hear were birds chirping.

FORTY-THREE

Matt tried to figure out where he was. The rough road they had taken here, and the near-total silence, meant he was somewhere in the country, but that was as much as he could narrow it down. His fingers brushed against the rough planking of the wall he was leaning against. There was a musty smell in the air. He guessed he was in a barn. An abandoned barn. There were probably hundreds of them near Snowden. There was no way anybody would find him before Burke came back.

A terrifying thought assailed him. What if Burke wasn't coming back? He'd said he would return to get the Cadillac, but he could have taken it with him. Would he really risk Matt going public with what he knew? Walter's car had been in his possession for over twenty years. Other people must have seen it. Why take the chance that somebody would remember the red flocking and come forward once Matt sounded the alarm?

Sonya would call him when she got back from the prison. She would suspect something had happened if he didn't respond, but she would have no reason to think Burke was involved, not when she had received a text from Matt's phone saying that the Cadillac in Burke's workshop wasn't Walter's. And even if she still suspected Burke, there was nothing to connect him to Matt's disappearance.

Burke could just wait it out, wait until the frenzy over Matt's disappearance died down, and then come back here and put his corpse somewhere where nobody would ever find it. Matt recalled from something he'd seen on TV that a human being could survive for ages without food, but that you couldn't last for more than a few days without water. After everything he'd been through, was it all going to end here? With him slowly dying of thirst? *I want to live*, he mutely screamed.

Matt sat in the darkness, hooded, for what seemed like hours. He felt as if he was in a sensory deprivation chamber. Time lost all meaning. Eventually the birds fell silent, signaling the arrival of nightfall. His mind began to play tricks on him. He found himself having conversations— with Emma, with his mom and dad, with Anthony—that felt real until the moment he realized they weren't.

He was telling Emma it would be a mistake for her to move to Saudi Arabia when he heard a car drive up. He ignored it, certain it was his imagination. "Women aren't allowed to drive there," he told Emma. "You'll have to walk everywhere, and it's a million degrees in the shade." A car door shut. Footsteps approached. Burke had come back. Matt felt absurdly grateful. Tears welled up in his eyes. He was going to live.

"Matt. Matt."

It was a woman's voice, not Burke's. His heart sank. He had imagined it.

The door creaked. A beam of light penetrated his hood.

"Matt! Thank God." The hood was yanked off his head. Sonya's face was illuminated by moonlight. She removed the tape from his mouth. "Are you all right?"

He took a couple of deep breaths. "I think so. It's you. It's really you."

"What happened?"

"Burke caught me at the house. He has a gun. We've got to get out of here before he comes back."

Sonya tried to rip the duct tape off Matt's ankles, but it wouldn't tear.

"I'll be right back," she said.

Matt looked around. He was in a rundown barn, as he'd suspected. Walter's Cadillac lay on the ground a few feet away, beside the duffel bag. Burke was planning to return after all.

Sonya returned with a pair of scissors. Matt explained what had happened while she cut the tape on his wrists and ankles. When she was done, he took his phone out of the duffel bag and took some photos to document the scene. He put the phone in his pocket and then put the model car in the duffel bag. "Let's go," he said, slinging the bag over his shoulder.

"Stop right there," a voice commanded when they got outside. Dan Burke stood a few feet away, his gun pointed at them. "Put the bag on the ground and lie down beside it. Both of you."

Matt dropped the bag. "You're too late," he said. "I emailed pictures of the car to Jesse."

"Nice try."

"See for yourself." Matt tossed his phone to Burke. The move caught Burke by surprise. He instinctively reached for the phone. Matt took two quick steps and launched himself at Burke, like a defensive back making a tackle in midfield. The gun went off. Matt felt the bullet whistle by his ear just before his shoulders hit Burke in the midsection. Burke grunted as he hit the ground. The gun dropped, but before Burke could reach for it, Matt was squatting on his chest, his knees pinning Burke's arms. He made a fist with his hand and cocked his arm.

"Don't hit me," Burke whimpered.

Matt thought of Walter and Gwen, their lives cut short by this pitiful creature lying under him. He thought of all the years Ray had spent in jail because of him. Fury rose inside him.

"It's over, Matt," Sonya said. "It's over."

"I know," Matt said.

Then he smashed Burke in the face with all his might.

"There's one thing I don't understand," Matt said after he and Sonya had tied up Burke with the duct tape. They were waiting for the police to arrive. "How did you know where to find me?"

"I tracked down your phone from your computer."

"But you can't log onto my computer without—"

"Statechamps. One word. Lower case," Sonya said. "Lamest password ever."

FORTY-FOUR

"Hot off the press," Matt's dad said, handing Matt the paper as he staggered into the living room the next morning, his body still stiff from the hours he had spent tied up on the barn floor.

Matt read the headline.

Mayor's Husband Charged with 21-Year-Old Double Murder
Former Falcons Star Player Turns Sleuth

Underneath was a photo of Dan Burke flanked by two cops, his eye black and swollen shut.

Matt lowered himself into a chair and began reading. The article took up all of the front page and a good chunk of page two as well. The reporter had interviewed Matt and Sonya after they left the police station the night before, and they had given him the entire story—with one minor omission. They had seen no need to muddy the waters by mentioning their initial belief that the Chief was the culprit.

"It reads like a thriller, doesn't it?" Matt's dad said when Matt put the paper down.

"It's definitely got a lot of fiction."

Matt barely recognized himself. The reporter had transformed him from a trembling teenager, petrified that he was going to die, into a fearless young man who had courageously handled a situation that would have challenged James Bond.

After breakfast Matt and Sonya went to see Jolene. Ray's grandmother was standing in the doorway of her room, dabbing at her eyes with a handkerchief. As soon as she saw them, she burst into tears.

Matt had read the expression *tears of joy* in books, but he'd never seen them in real life until now. They must have been contagious, because Sonya started crying too. It wasn't long before Matt's eyes welled up as well.

The three embraced. "Ray's coming home," Jolene said over and over, as if the news hadn't quite sunk in.

After they said goodbye to Jolene, Matt and Sonya dropped by the Justice Project office. There had been a couple of developments with the case, and Jesse and Angela brought them up to date.

Dan Burke had pled guilty to the murders and accepted a life sentence with no possibility of parole. Matt felt a twinge of disappointment. This was one time when he wouldn't have had a problem with the death penalty. Jamie Jenkins had held a live press conference to explain her involvement in the hit-and-run and to announce that she was resigning as mayor of Snowden.

"She took full responsibility for not reporting the accident. She could have blamed Burke—she was so young at the time—but she didn't," Angela said.

Jamie had been waiting for Walter when he came to work the morning after the hit-and-run. When he asked about the damage to the car, she told him she had driven into a parking meter. She said her dad would go ballistic if he found out she'd taken the car without permission, and Walter agreed to cover for her.

"Remember when Jamie said how kind Walter had been?" Sonya recalled. "That's what she was talking about."

They knew the rest of the story. Walter went home, read the article in the *Sentinel* and realized Jamie had lied to him. That's when he made the call to Burke, a call that ended up costing him and Gwen their lives, and Ray his freedom.

"Jamie seemed relieved that it was all out in the open," Angela said. "Imagine living with that for all these years."

"Is she going to get charged?" Matt asked.

"No," Jesse said. "It happened too long ago. The state has to file charges within a few years from the time a crime is committed. Except for murder. There's no time limit there. That's why they can still charge Burke."

"They should put Burke in Ray's cell," Matt said.

"Now that would be justice," Jesse agreed.

★ ★ ★

Three weeks later Matt and Sonya sat beside Jolene in a Snowden courtroom jammed with Ray's supporters. A huge cheer erupted when the judge apologized to Ray, on behalf of the state, for his wrongful conviction and told him he was free to go.

Words couldn't begin to describe the joy in Jolene's face when Ray wrapped her in an embrace. She held on to him like a drowning person clutching a life preserver.

Everybody started crying. Even Jesse had tears rolling down his face.

A mob of reporters swarmed Ray when he came outside, thrusting microphones in his face. Someone shouted out the one question reporters never seem to tire of asking.

"How do you feel?"

"I feel great," Ray said with a big smile. He summoned Matt and Sonya to join him and told the crowd he owed his freedom to them. He stood between them and raised their arms in the air in a victory salute. Ray's supporters clapped and cheered.

Ray was asked what he was going to do with the $420,000 the state was paying him in compensation—$20,000 for each year he had been in jail. He didn't bother mentioning the obvious—that no amount of money could compensate for the years he'd lost. The first thing he was going to do, he said, was find a nice apartment for him and Jolene. Then he was going to buy back his dad's model-car collection from Ralph Ellison.

Then he and Jolene got into a car and went to the cemetery so he could finally pay his respects to his mother and father, twenty-one years after they had died.

A reporter cornered Matt. "How does this compare to winning the state championship?"

Matt caught Sonya's eye. She burst out laughing. They'd just restored a man's freedom, and this fool was wondering how it compared to winning a football game. Snowden was never going to change. Matt resisted the urge to mock the reporter. Instead, he answered the question honestly. "Winning the championship was special, but this is even better."

The reporter had one more question. "How do you feel?"

Matt looked him in the eye. "How much time do you have?"

Author's Note

Jesse Donovan's wrongful conviction for the murder of two men is based on the true story of Larry Hicks.

In 1978 Hicks, a nineteen-year-old man living in Gary, Indiana, was convicted of two counts of murder and sentenced to death. At his trial he was represented by a public defender who failed to examine both the dark-red stains on Hicks's jeans that the prosecutor claimed were blood and the knife he said was the murder weapon. Two weeks before Hicks's scheduled execution, a volunteer lawyer took over his case. He proved that the supposed bloodstains on Hicks's jeans were rust stains, and that the knife was too short to have been the murder weapon. The two eyewitnesses who claimed they had seen Hicks threatening the victim admitted they had lied because they were afraid of the real killer. Hicks was found not guilty at a second trial and released from jail after serving two years on death row.

Bill Matheson's wrongful conviction for the murder of his wife is based on the true story of Michael Morton.

In 1987 Morton, a supermarket manager in Texas, was convicted of murdering his wife, Christine, and sentenced to life in prison. Eighteen years later, in 2005, Morton's new lawyers applied for DNA testing of a bloody bandanna that had been found on a construction site one hundred yards from the Mortons' home the day after the murder. (At the time, neither the prosecution nor Morton's original lawyers thought it had any connection to the case.)

The district attorney claimed that a DNA test would "muddy the waters" and fought the motion in the courts for five years before a judge finally ordered the test. The test revealed that the blood of Christine Morton was on the bandanna, along with the DNA of Mark Alan Norwood, a drifter with a long criminal record. In 2013 Norwood was convicted of killing Christine Morton. At the request of Michael Morton and the rest of Christine's family, Norwood's prosecutor agreed not to seek the death penalty, and Norwood was sentenced to life in prison.

Michael Morton was released in 2012, after serving twenty-five years in prison. He had been denied parole in 2007 because he refused to lie and falsely admit he had killed his wife.

The Justice Project is a fictional organization, but similar real-life organizations exist in many states and provinces and around the world, fighting on behalf of the wrongly convicted. The Innocence Network (innocencenetwork.org) has a list of these organizations and more information.

At the time this book was written, over 2,250 falsely convicted men and women had been exonerated in the United States since 1989. Visit the National Registry of Exonerations (law.umich.edu/special/exoneration) for details.

There have been 162 death-row exonerations in the United States since 1973. Information is available at the Death Penalty Information Center website, deathpenaltyinfo.org.

ACKNOWLEDGMENTS

I would like to express my gratitude to the many people who helped me during the writing of this book. First, thank you to my family and friends who read the manuscript and whose feedback was invaluable: my wife, Claudette Jaiko; my daughter, Laura Betcherman; and my good friends Jake Onrot, David Diamond and Bill Kelly. Special thanks go to my publisher, Ruth Linka, my wonderful editor, Sara Cassidy, and the rest of the team at Orca Book Publishers. And a huge thank-you to my agent, Amy Tompkins at Transatlantic Agency, for her faith in me and in my story.

MICHAEL BETCHERMAN is an award-winning author and screenwriter. He is the author of the young adult mystery novels *Breakaway* and *Face-Off*, both published by Penguin Canada. *Breakaway* was a finalist for the John Spray Mystery Award. *Face-Off* was short-listed for the Arthur Ellis Best Juvenile/YA Book Award. Michael has numerous writing credits in both dramatic and documentary television. He is also the author/creator of the groundbreaking online novels *The Daughters of Freya* and *Suzanne*. Michael lives in Toronto with his wife, Claudette Jaiko.